VOLUNTEER FOR MURDER

By Tim Myers

Volunteer for Murder
by Tim Myers.

Copyright © 2011 Tim Myers

All rights reserved.

This is a work of fiction. Names, characters, places, and incidents either are the product of the author's imagination or are used fictitiously, and any resemblance to actual persons, living or dead, business establishments, events, or locales is entirely coincidental.

No part of this book may be reproduced, scanned, or distributed in any printed or electronic form without permission. Please do not participate in or encourage piracy of copyrighted materials in violation of the author's rights.

Dedication

To Emily

Chapter 1

At first glance, it appeared that Vera Skyles Hobart was drunk as she staggered into the Jackson's Ferry Soup Kitchen, knocking over a gray metal chair at one table and sending a basket of day-old bread to the floor from atop another. It wasn't until she fell to the floor that the reason for her erratic behavior became readily apparent; her groping hands had partially obscured a short-handled knife with the spreading jaws of a rattlesnake mounted on its haft. The blade was driven to the hilt into her chest, though there was surprisingly little blood staining the front of her black and white Christian Dior suit from last year's line. As Seth Jackson and Gillian Graywolf rushed toward her from the soup kitchen's serving line, Vera's manicured fingers abruptly stopped fighting for purchase, slipped away from the haft and slid lifelessly to the floor.

A half hour before Vera's deadly entrance, it had been just another typical day of volunteer work at the Jackson's Ferry Soup Kitchen.
As Seth Jackson finished cutting the oversized sourdough buns donated by a local burger house into individual servings, he watched his love Gillian Graywolf deposit dollops of fruit cocktail into small, sterile green bowls. He still found it hard to believe he was with her, even after two years of being together. His equal or better in every way he cared to count, Gillian stood a half inch taller than his own six feet, but where he was built with a stocky, solid frame, Gillian was more like a swan, long and lithe, blessed with the grace of a dancer; her every move was pure elegance. Her lustrous straight coal-black hair cropped at the shoulder and her copper skin revealed the Catawba Indian side of her heritage, while a most startling pair of pale blue eyes marked the Irish in her; it was a wonderfully exotic combination of

DNA that never failed to leave Seth breathless. Gillian was the daughter of a cop, something that gave them a lot in common since Seth had spent several years on the Charlotte police force himself. She had an analytical way of looking at the world that matched Seth's own perspective, though the two of them varied wildly on many of their opinions as to how that world should be run. It certainly made for some interesting conversations.

Gillian looked up from her task and noticed Seth watching her. With a gentle smile, she said, "I appreciate the attention as much as the next lady, but don't you think you'd better concentrate on that knife blade?"

Seth shrugged. "Nancy Kenshaw's working the infirmary today. If I'm going to have an accident, I couldn't be in better hands."

Gillian came to him and gently removed the blade from his grasp. "Let's not give the poor child any more reason to pine over you than she already has."

"Now what fun is that? And you know as well as I do that the 'poor child' is almost thirty."

As Gillian helped him stack the cut portions of bread into a large warming tray, she said, "Anybody born after Kennedy's assassination is robbing the cradle for you. She probably wasn't even alive in '69 for the moon landing."

Seth took her lightly in his arms. "You don't have to worry about me. I'm already involved with someone special."

"Anyone I know?"

Seth smiled. "You two are very close."

Gillian favored him with a quick kiss as Mattie Medlin, the Soup Kitchen's supervisor, flicked them both lightly with her dishtowel. Mattie, a petite black woman who kept the kitchen as antiseptic as an operating room, said with a shake of her head, "Look at the two of you, both in your forties and carrying on like teenagers. You should be ashamed of yourselves."

Seth broke away, then tweaked Mattie on the cheek.

"You're just jealous, Mattie, admit it."

She pretended to study him for a moment, then said, "Sorry, Seth, you're a little skinny for my tastes."

Gillian said, "Don't encourage him, Mattie. I'm trying to get him to drop those extra fifteen pounds he's so fond of."

Seth grabbed the cook's hands and said, "At last, a woman who can appreciate me for what I am."

She shooed him with her rag and said, "Enough of your foolishness, Seth. You two grab a plate, we're all getting ready to eat."

The meal arrangement had surprised Seth when he'd first started volunteering at the soup kitchen a few years earlier; the workers who served the food ate the same offerings that went to the people they waited on. The fare was always healthy and hearty, and Mattie possessed a gift of making even the most common menu tasty.

As they filled their plates from the selection of ham, mashed potatoes, fruit cocktail, green beans and the bread Seth had cut, he and Gillian took their trays to the volunteer table. There was an unwritten rule that the full-time staff occupied one table while the volunteers shared another. Seth and Gillian had been a part of the first shift set-up crew, and glancing at his watch, he saw that the other two volunteers for the day were both late.

Just as he was about to ask Gillian about the absences, a plump harried woman in gray slacks and a faded maroon blouse rushed in.

"Sorry I'm late, everybody. Wes Junior didn't want to go to his Grandma's house, goodness knows why, and I had a devil of a time getting him out of his car seat." Christy James spoke in a rapid fire delivery as she slipped on an apron and heaped her plate with food.

Gillian asked, "How do you have time to come here with three kids, one of them still in diapers?"

Christy smiled lightly. "Well, it gets me out of the house." A little louder, she added, "And you know I can't miss Mattie's cooking, can I?"

Mattie's head lifted as her name was spoken. "Christy, you're not going to get on my good side by slinging compliments around. We need to depend on you being here."

Christy managed to look contrite, then noticed that there was still a missing volunteer. "At least it looks like I'm not the last one in."

Mattie shook her head. "I know, I checked the schedule. Vera Hobart's working the late shift with you. I don't understand it, Vera's always so regular when she comes to help out."

Christy sat beside Gillian and heartily dug into her meal. Between bites, in a low voice meant only for her fellow volunteers, Christy said, "It's no wonder Vera's late. From what I've been hearing, it's amazing she has the nerve to show up at all."

Seth was surprised by the comment. He'd come to know Christy well over the years in the course of his volunteer work, and it was the first time he'd ever heard her say anything remotely gossipy. "What in particular have you heard?"

Christy frowned. "You know I don't believe in sharing bad news, but I hear Vera's been having male visitors at home in the middle of the day, and her supposedly such a good Christian woman."

Gillian said, "Maybe she and her husband decided to spice up their marriage a little. It's been known to happen."

Christy raised an eyebrow. "You obviously don't know Bradley Hobart. He's not the lunch romance type." In a voice almost too low to hear, she added, "At least not with his wife." She was immediately embarrassed by what she'd said. "Now that's fine Christian charity, isn't it? I know better than to speculate in idle gossip. Forgive me, you two, it's been a tough couple of days. Wes Junior hates to be out of my sight, Charlie's having trouble with a bully at school and Sarah's started wearing black all the time." Christy brushed a strand of straw blond hair out of her face. "So tell me, have you two come up with a date yet?" She was always after Seth about when he and Gillian were going to get married.

Seth winked at Gillian as he said, "We were just discussing it when you came in."

Christy's eyes went wide, and for a moment she forgot about the plate of food in front of her. "It's about time. And what did you two come up with?"

Seth smiled brightly. "We're both pretty sure it's the ninth of April."

Christy said excitedly, "Why that's today."

Gillian leaned across the table and tweaked Seth's arm. "See? I told you."

Christy said, "You're getting married today? After you volunteer together? That's so romantic."

Seth looked at her in mock surprise. "Married? Who said anything about marriage? We just weren't sure about the date. Thanks for straightening us out."

Christy eyes narrowed. "Seth Jackson, you're pulling my leg. And here I thought you two were about to make things right between the two of you."

Seth patted Gillian's hand as he said, "Christy, things have never been more right."

Gillian laughed gently as she took her plate to the dishwashing station, Seth following close behind. She said, "What's so wrong about not being married?"

"We're in a small town in North Carolina," Seth replied. "You're not supposed to have sex unless you're married, and I'm pretty sure everybody knows we've been having it."

"I'd like to have a little now, myself," Gillian said.

"I don't think Mattie would approve."

She laughed softly. "In that case, how about a rain check? I'm free after we're through here."

As Seth nodded his agreement, he said, "It's a date."

Mattie joined them at the line. "Don't just stand there making time, we've got hungry people to feed." She clapped her hands together and in a louder voice, said, "Finish up, people. The doors open in three minutes."

Christy said, "But what about Vera?"

"Darlin, I can't spend my life wondering about the people who don't show up. Gillian, you and Seth handle the counter. Christy, you'll be our hostess today. Let's go."

As Seth and Gillian found their places behind the steaming tubs of food, Mattie said, "You two have done this enough before. Think you can handle two stations apiece?"

Gillian said, "Open the doors, Mattie. Seth and I can handle it."

"I like your spirit, girl."

Seth and Gillian prepared a few servings before the doors opened, speedily putting large portions of everything onto the plates. This was the only hot meal most of the people coming in would have for the day, and that was one thing about Mattie that never wavered; no one ever left the Soup Kitchen hungry for more.

As the doors opened, Ace was the first in line, as was his custom. Known only as 'Ace' to everyone around town, the older man was dressed in faded clothes, patched and darned in several places, and sported a beard that was more salt than pepper. Still, Seth found a regal quality to the man, a pride in the way he carried himself that made him think that Ace had once been Somebody in the real world. It was most likely one of the three or four prototypical stories of their clientele, a successful person driven to the streets by an addiction to alcohol, drugs or gambling. They fell as far as they could, and too few of them ever managed to pull themselves back up. That was one thing he liked about Ace. Though it was obvious he'd fallen farther than most people could imagine, the man had managed to retain something of his dignity.

Ace smiled with perfect straight teeth as he said, "Pile the plate high, Seth. I'm in the mood for some of Mattie's good cooking."

As Gillian loaded another plate with food, she asked, "Where's Penny today?"

Seth knew that Ace and the woman known as Penny were

frequent diners together at the soup kitchen. He had no idea what the woman's real name was, either. Ace had once told her Penny'd gotten her nickname because she was so small, hardly bigger than a penny, he'd said with a laugh. It was a common practice for the people who came in to use names other than the ones they'd been born with. Seth knew Gillian herself had changed last names a few times, from Hurley, the name she'd been born with, to Kerner from her ex-husband, and finally to Graywolf, taken from her maternal grandmother.

Ace shrugged in response to the question. "Don't know. She didn't show up at her place in line. I'm sure she'll be in later."

As he took the plate, he said graciously, "Thanks for coming out today."

Seth smiled. "No place else we'd rather be."

As the regulars flowed through the line, most of them with brief greetings to Seth and Gillian along the way, the volunteers worked in steady unison filling the plates with food. There was a good crowd, about thirty-five through the line for first servings before Mattie called out to the crowd, "It's time for seconds, if anybody wants them. We're all out of meat, but there's plenty of vegetables to go around if anybody's still hungry."

About two thirds of the patrons took advantage of the additional offering of food, and by the time they were ready to shut down the line, the once-large portions in the pots were low enough to transfer the remainders into small plastic gallon containers. Seth was moving the last of the green beans so one of the regular workers could wash out the tub when he heard a disturbance at the door.

As Vera Hobart stumbled in, Seth dropped the container on the counter and raced to help her, Gillian a half step behind.

By the time they got to her, it looked as if it was already too late.

Chapter 2

Gillian knelt beside Vera, shouting for Nancy Kenshaw as she searched for a pulse she suspected she wouldn't find, while Seth went to the Soup Kitchen's telephone and called for an ambulance. Gillian liked to tease Seth about Nancy's obvious attraction to him, but she was glad the registered nurse was working in the attached free clinic that day. Gillian had taken the basic Red Cross course on CPR, but she'd never learned how to deal with a life-threatening knife wound. In seconds, Nancy brushed her out of the way, and Gillian stood with Seth. He wrapped one arm around her protectively, and she nestled closer to him as they watched Nancy work.

Though the circumstances were dire, Gillian felt herself drawing from Seth's strength as they stood there together. Seth was attractive enough, but he'd never be called handsome; his nose had been broken a few too many times, and there was a sizable scar that ran from the center of his chin to the left side of his neck. She'd asked him about it when they'd first started dating, and he'd laughingly told her he'd cut himself shaving. Only after stumbling across an old article in the newspaper did she discover that he'd been wounded by a dangerous suspect as he'd been arresting him. Seth didn't like to talk much about his former career as a cop, his time before that as a college instructor, and most of all, his first wife Melissa. She'd died unexpectedly around the time Seth had been shot on the job, but that was all Gillian really knew about it. The wounds, to his leg as well as his heart, had forced Seth into an early retirement that had altered the course of his life forever. Gillian knew that when Seth was ready to talk about his past, he would. The only thing he ever said was that all of it was a lifetime ago, almost as though it had happened to another person. Gillian knew a good man when she saw one; she could afford to wait until he felt ready to tell her. For now, she was perfectly happy to share each day of their lives together without questioning the past or what the future might hold.

Several of the Soup Kitchen patrons were heading for the door when Seth called out, "Why don't you all go back to your seats? I'm sorry, but the police will need statements from everyone before you can go." Several of the clients were not on the best of terms with the local police, and a grumbling started among them. Seth held up his hands and said, "You were all here eating, so none of you could have done this; you've got forty witnesses. Wouldn't you rather the police know that up front?"

A few hurried nods and the crowd quickly settled back down at their tables. Gillian admired the way Seth had with people from all walks of life; he knew how to get through to just about anyone.

Gillian asked Nancy, "Is there anything we can do?"

"There's nothing anybody can do. I'm afraid Vera's beyond help. Did anyone call an ambulance?"

Seth nodded. "I'd better call the police, too."

As Seth moved to the telephone, a frequent diner named Wizard left his seat to get a better look at the body. Gillian put a light hand on his arm and said, "I wouldn't get too close to her."

Wizard pointed a dirty finger at Vera's chest. "All I want to know is what in the world is that woman doing with Penny's knife in her chest?"

The mention of his friend's name brought Ace forward, who'd been standing in the background with some of the other diners. He peered closer at the blade and said, "Surely you don't think Penny had anything to do with this. She won't even step on an ant if she can help it."

Wizard held up his hands. "I'm not saying anything, but that's her knife and you know it, Ace." The grizzled old man looked defiant.

Ace said quickly, "She lost that knife a couple of days ago. Penny had it for protection, and she was upset about losing it."

    Seth rejoined them, listening silently to the conversation. That was another thing Gillian loved about him; whenever anyone spoke, he really listened, instead of planning what he was going to say next.

    With a serious tone in his voice, he said, "Ace, you'd better be absolutely certain Penny told you that before you share that story to the police."

    The man's normally jovial side was gone, replaced by a steel glare. "That's the way it happened, Seth. You let me worry about it, okay? The last I heard, you weren't a cop anymore, so I don't see that it's any of your business."

    Seth held up his hands. "Just trying to help. Do you have any idea where Penny is now? The police will want to talk with her."

    Ace said testily, "I said I didn't know where she was, and that still stands. You know her, Seth, she wouldn't hurt anybody, let alone use that knife."

    Gillian said softly, "It's her knife, Ace. Nobody's denying that part of it."

    "For God's sake, it was for protection, though I doubt she would have ever used it, even to save herself. You're a woman, you should understand. Then again, probably not. You've never spent a day of your life out in the streets, with no one to care whether you live or die."

    Seth stepped forward. "Easy, Ace. We're here to help, remember? Why don't we all just relax until we can hear what Penny has to say about this." Still, Gillian couldn't help but agree with what Ace said.

    As Seth spoke, a siren in the background became more intense as it approached. The soup kitchen was in the lower downtown district where the homeless and hungry congregated. It was close enough to the emergency services of an EMS unit to merit the prompt response. As the attendants rushed inside with their kits, Seth could hear the police siren close behind. Due to the repeated troubles in that section of town, the police were also notoriously quick to

respond.
 Before they could arrive, though, the EMS attendants were vainly trying to revive Vera. Nancy Kenshaw had been right; Vera was beyond anyone's help.
 Ten seconds later, a pair of uniformed cops walked in, scanned the room, then walked directly to Seth. Though he'd been a cop in Charlotte, a city that was a good hour and a half away, nearly everyone on the force knew his history and counted him as a friend.
 Luke Jenkins, the older of the two policemen, said, "There's always some excitement around you, isn't there?"
 Seth shrugged. "It's a curse, what can I say."
 Jenkins nodded toward the body. "Tell me about it."
 "Her name's Vera Hobart. We were just finishing up on the serving line when she stumbled in. Before she could say a word, she was gone."
 "See anybody outside?" the other cop asked.
 Seth shook his head. "There are at least a dozen ways somebody could be out of sight before Vera even made it through the front door."
 "Would it have hurt to look?"
 Seth, ignoring the hostile glare of the cop, said, "It was a judgment call." He stuck out his hand. "The name's Seth Jackson."
 Grudgingly, the man took his hand. "Bart Lancing."
 Jenkins said, "Now that you two have made friends, why don't we start getting statements from these lowlifes."
 With a trace of steel in his voice, Seth said, "We call them patrons."
 Jenkins held up his hands. "Sorry." He turned to his partner. "Officer Lancing, why don't you go take statements from these 'patrons' and see if anyone saw anything."
 Lancing nodded and moved toward the diners. Seth started after him when Jenkins put a restraining hand on his shoulder. "Where are you going? We're not done talking."
 "I want to make sure Lancing's polite to our guests."
 They held each other's stares for a moment, then Gillian

broke the tension. "Seth didn't see anything I didn't. I can answer any questions you've got."

Jenkins looked at her for a moment, then said, "You're Frank Hurley's daughter, aren't you?"

Gillian was still surprised when people recognized her because of her father. Frank Hurley had been dead ten years, but his reputation as the finest cop Jackson's Ferry had ever seen lived long after he had. Cancer had slowly eaten away at him, stealing his life away one breath at a time. It was the one evil Frank Hurley had not been able to beat. His lingering death had been one of the reasons Gillian had changed her life, scaling back her stock brokerage practice to the point where she could spend her time the way she wanted, not just the way people expected of her. Though her limited business dealings cut her income to a modest amount, it provided the opportunity for her to volunteer while still allowing her enough time to enjoy her life, one moment at time. It was a decision she would have gladly made over again every time she greeted a new day. The first place she'd volunteered had been at the Jackson's Ferry Hospice, trying to ease the suffering of others going through the losing battle her own father had fought so valiantly.

Gillian smiled at the reference to her father. "Yes, I'm Frankie's girl."

Waving Seth away, he said, "You'll do just fine, Ma'am."

Gillian watched as Seth joined the other policeman, and wished she could listen in on the fun. Seth knew the law, having taught Criminal Justice at UNC Charlotte as well as spent time enforcing it later on the streets of the Queen City. Officer Lancing had better watch every word that came out of his mouth.

Gillian said, "I don't know what I can tell you Seth didn't. We saw her stagger in, and by the time we got to her, she was dead."

There was a commotion where Lancing was questioning the patrons, and Gillian clearly heard Wizard say, "I'm telling you, it's Penny's knife. I told Seth and now I'm telling you."

Officer Jenkins suddenly lost interest in Gillian and moved to Wizard. She followed closely behind.

"What's going on?" the cop asked.

Before Lancing could explain, Wizard said, "It's Penny's knife, I don't care what anybody says." At that, he glared at Ace.

"I'm not denying it. All I'm saying is Penny told me it was stolen a few days ago."

Jenkins held up a hand for silence. "Let me talk to this Penny woman and we'll straighten this all out."

Ace looked defiantly at the older cop. "She's not here. Nobody's seen her today."

Jenkins said, "Then maybe we'd better start looking for her. I'll need a complete description of her, where she hangs out, things like that."

"That's the problem," Seth said. "This time of day, she's always right here."

After the police took the names of everyone present at the soup kitchen, including the volunteers and regular workers, they sent everyone on their way.

Seth and Gillian lingered in back while the police finished photographing the body and videotaping just about everything else inside as well as outside the building. Mattie came back with a harried look on her face. "This is going to hurt, people. I'm not sure how our donors are going to feel about one of my volunteers being killed inside the soup kitchen. I've got a suspicion we're about to enter a dry spell for contributions. I don't even want to think about what it's going to take to get another volunteer down here."

Seth put a hand on Mattie's shoulder. "If you need us, we'll work every day until this is straightened out. As for donors, Gillian and I have a lot of friends in the community. We'll make sure they know none of this was the soup kitchen's fault."

Mattie wiped a single tear out of the corner of her eye. "Bless you both, but how can I be certain Vera didn't get killed because she was in the wrong neighborhood? Most of our people aren't violent, but you know as well as I do that some of them have been in and out of mental institutions half their lives. I don't doubt we've got a few ex-cons, too, but my lands, that's who we're here to help, people who can't help themselves."

Gillian said, "You can't blame yourself, Mattie."

"Gillian, my shoulders are big enough to carry the weight, they've got to be. I'd give anything to erase what happened here, but people will still be hungry come tomorrow, and I'm going to feed them as long as I've got food to put out and folks to help me serve it."

"That's the spirit. Do you need any more help back here in the kitchen?"

"No," Mattie said as she unconsciously took a sweep of her rag across the already pristine counter. "We'll be working hard to clean the place up as soon as the police are through."

"I'll find out how much longer they're going to be. With any luck, you'll be back in business tomorrow, and if your scheduled volunteers don't want to come in, give us a call, you've got our numbers."

Mattie placed a hand on each of their shoulders. "Bless the both of you."

Seth and Gillian made their way out front in time to see Vera's body being loaded into the back of the ambulance. There was a small crowd of spectators watching, and Gillian scanned the crowd, searching for Penny without luck. The day was a little breezy for May, but the sun managed to warm her despite the steady wind. Late Spring was in all its glory, but the beauty of the weather was lost on her. Vera's death had managed to take that away, at least for the moment. Back inside, it was hard to tell that anything had happened once the body was moved; the knife had acted as a stopper, keeping most of Vera's blood from spilling to the floor. The forensic team had finished up with the photographic and video records inside and had moved to the exterior.

Jenkins looked up as they approached. "You two still here? I thought I told everyone to leave."

"We had some work to do in the kitchen. Any idea when Mattie can have her place back?"

Jenkins shrugged. "The chief's on his way. It's his decision, but I can't imagine us being more than another hour outside, and we're already done in here."

Gillian asked, "Has anybody seen Penny yet?"

The cop shook his head. "I sent Lancing out to look, but I doubt he's having much luck. There are too many places to hide around here, and this Penny probably knows them all."

As he spoke, a large barrel-chested man came in, sporting a shiny badge hanging from his front jacket pocket. It was obvious at one time in his life he'd been physically fit, but his hours behind a desk and too many hearty meals had softened him around the edges. Hair cropped military-short, Sheriff Harley Kline had spent twenty years as an MP before retiring to North Carolina. He'd quickly grown bored with civilian life and had run for sheriff; Kline was on his fourth term, and from the look of things, he'd be the county sheriff until the fattening food he loved finally killed him.

He and Seth were friends, though there was something about the man Gillian didn't take to. He was too severe for the small town of Jackson's Ferry, still too spit-and-polish for her tastes. Her father had been twice the lawman Kline was, but he'd always had an easy, good-natured air about him that even the criminals he arrested seemed to respond to.

Kline tipped his head to Gillian, then said to Seth, "It figures you'd be here."

Seth replied, "Purely a coincidence."

"Now Seth, you know I don't believe in coincidences."

Jenkins stepped forward. "Sir, I've got a full report here for you."

"Bring me up to date, son."

Jenkins' eyes went to Seth and Gillian as he hesitated. Impatiently, the sheriff said, "Officer, I asked for the highlights, and I'd like to have them."

Jenkins' fingers tightened on his notebook as he started his oral report. "From eyewitness accounts and the physical evidence, the victim, Vera Hobart, was stabbed just outside the door and staggered inside. Nobody we talked to saw a thing before she came in, and the coroner says she couldn't have walked far with that blade in her."

"Was she robbed?"

"No, her purse was still on her shoulder, and there was seventy dollars inside. It's hard to tell if any jewelry's missing. We didn't find any rings or necklaces on her."

Kline rubbed his chin. "So it looks like another random act of violence."

"Not necessarily," Jenkins said. "One of the soup kitchen 'patrons'," he looked at Seth as he said the last word, "claims the murder weapon belongs to a street woman named Penny. I've got Lancing out looking for her now."

Seth added, "One of her friends claims the knife was stolen."

Kline laughed roughly. "Now why am I not surprised? Well, it doesn't look like there's anything I can do here at the moment. Thanks, Jenkins." The officer took the dismissal and headed outside. Kline turned to Seth and Gillian. "Now what are you two still doing here?"

"We were just leaving."

Kline took a step toward Seth, and in a voice nearly too low for Gillian to hear, asked, "Do you have any ideas why somebody would want this woman dead?"

"Sorry, I don't have a clue."

Kline tapped him on the shoulder. "You're getting soft, buddy."

Seth responded by patting the sheriff lightly on the belly. "There's a lot of that going around."

Kline laughed as they left. It wasn't until they were back at Seth's pickup truck that Gillian spoke. "Do you really think Vera's murder was just some random act of violence?"

"I don't know, that's sure what it looks like. Maybe she was just in the wrong place at the wrong time."

"Don't tell me you think Penny actually could have killed her."

As Seth drove away, he said, "I'll admit she doesn't seem the type. I've known Penny a few years, and I'm well aware of her attitude toward killing anything." He shook his head, then added, "Ace said her knife was stolen, but I'm not sure I believe him; he could easily be lying to help a friend. All in all, though, I'd have to say I'm inclined to think she's innocent."

"So what do we do now?"

Seth smiled. "I seem to remember a rain check I'm ready to cash. We're a good twenty minutes from my farm. Why don't we go to your loft?"

Gillian smiled. "You're still interested after what just happened?"

He put an arm around her. "There's nothing we can do about Vera. As for being interested, what do you think?"

Gillian nestled close to him. "So why are you driving five miles under the speed limit? Let's go."

Chapter 3

Afterward, as they lay entwined in Gillian's bed, Seth looked around the loft Gillian called home. A space that had once housed a small textile mill, her loft was one of ten units that had been converted into living spaces. Seth knew Gillian loved the wide openness of the apartment; the high ceilings of stained wood, large scarred beams that supported the structure, and the pipes and ducts running under them painted in stark shades of white. The hardwood floors that had suffered under the heavy load of people and working machinery sported the patina wood develops only after years of use and abuse. There was no set floor-plan for the loft, and Gillian delighted in moving the furniture to match her mood. Only the kitchen and bathroom spaces were anchored in one corner, leaving the rest of the space an open palette for Gillian's creative whims. Screens, both silk and stained glass, were easily rearranged to modify the layout, though Gillian normally just kept the entire 2,500 square feet open. Their choice of living spaces was one reason Seth and Gillian had never brought up the possibility of living together. Where Gillian's loft was not much more than wide open space, Seth's own home was modest by anyone's definition, a little less than a thousand-square-foot one bedroom cottage in the center of his small Christmas tree farm. He'd bought the farm after his early retirement, hoping it would be a haven for him to get away from his past. Grady West, the farm's only employee, often boasted that his double-wide trailer was bigger than Seth's house, but it suited him perfectly. Seth knew and loved every inch of his living space, and any more room would have driven him crazy.

Gillian rubbed a hand on his bare chest. "What are you thinking about?"

He looked down at her soft curves, tracing the line from her bare hip to her waist and up to her exposed breast with a light touch.

In mock surprise, she said, "Again? I thought men your age needed more rest."

As he moved his body to her, he said, "Forty-three is not that old."

Gillian sighed softly as she turned toward him. "So you're proving."

Seth was getting dressed when he heard someone pounding on Gillian's front door. Quickly buckling his belt, he called out to her, "Do you want me to get that?"

She came out of the bathroom in her robe. "Unless you want me to give somebody a cheap thrill."

He patted her bottom lightly as he walked past her to the door. "There's nothing cheap from where I stand. Anyway, I want you to save all of those for me."

Seth checked through the peephole before opening the door and was surprised to see Ace standing outside.

Opening the door, Seth asked, "What are you doing here, Ace? I didn't think you were too happy with us."

"I talked to your man Grady on the telephone, and he told me you were probably here. We need to talk. I'm sorry to bother you, but it can't wait."

Gillian came out in a pair of black slacks and a light gray lamb's wool sweater. "Come in, Ace. Can I get you something to drink?"

He nodded. "A cup of coffee would be great."

Gillian smiled before heading off to the kitchen. Somehow, she always managed to surprise Seth. Many of the volunteers, no matter how giving and gracious, would have been thrown off balance by one of the soup kitchen's clientele showing up on their doorstep, but Gillian reacted exactly as if she'd invited Ace herself.

Seth and Ace moved to the small dining table. Seth studied the homeless man. Ace was slightly embarrassed by his presence in Gillian's loft, that much was readily apparent as his hands fidgeted with his clothes. But beneath that, there was an underlying drive that had caused him to swallow his pride and seek Seth and Gillian's help; of course, that was it. Ace wasn't used to asking for help from anyone. Seth knew that from his previous contacts with the man. Probably the only thing that would drive him to violate his independence was a friend in trouble.

Seth said, "I know you're worried about Penny, but I'm not sure there's anything we can do until somebody finds her."

Ace grinned with those perfect white teeth, a smile that was out of place with the rest of his appearance. "You must have been one whale of a detective. You're right, that's why I'm here. The police are going to railroad Penny straight to jail if we don't do something about it."

Gillian came in carrying a tray with three mugs of coffee and a platter of cookies. Seth knew the treats had to have come from the bakery; Gillian's idea of cooking was warming something up in the microwave. Seth, on the other hand, loved to cook but hated cleaning up. Gillian was willing to take on that responsibility, and when the two of them weren't dining out at one of the interesting eating establishments Jackson's Ferry was blessed with, it made a perfect arrangement for them.

Gillian sat in one of the empty chairs, curling her long legs under her with an easy grace. Seth knew if he tried to sit that way it would take a team of chiropractors to unfold him. She took a sip of coffee and said, "Ace, Seth's retired from the force, and I've never even been a cop. What makes you think we can help?"

Ace said, "Gillian, everybody knows you're your father's little girl, and Frank Hurley was the best cop this town's ever seen. Seth's a retired cop and criminal justice professor, for God's sake. How can you not help Penny? I thought you two were big on volunteerism." He pushed away from the table and stood up. "Or is that just for show? Do you two really want to help the poor, or do you just want to do it when it's convenient for you?"

Seth said calmly, "If you thought that, you wouldn't be here, now would you? Enough of the histrionics. Why don't you sit back down and tell us what you have in mind."

Instead of doing as he asked, Ace began to pace around the kitchen area as he spoke. "I don't know where else to turn. Think about it. What better way to divert suspicion from yourself in a murder case than to frame a homeless woman? She's got no money for any decent defense or private detectives to prove she's innocent, and she's got the worst credibility of any defendant in the world. Penny doesn't have a permanent address, she lives on the street for God's sake. The district attorney's going to have a field day with that."

"As much as you hate to admit it, isn't there a chance Penny did it?" Gillian asked softly. "I've seen her in some pretty unusual moods over the past few months."

"So she had a few bad times. Does that make her a killer?"

Gillian continued, "Maybe Penny was having another one of those days today."

Ace said in a pleading voice, "But what if she wasn't?" He turned to Seth. "I know you don't believe me, but it's true what I said. Penny told me someone stole her knife. You have to see it's at least a possibility. I know her better than anyone else, and I'm telling you, Penny couldn't have killed Vera Hobart any more than the two of you could."

"I admit, we were just discussing that. It does seem highly unlikely she'd attack Vera Hobart. So if she's innocent, where is she?" Seth asked.

"Listen, on the streets, you learn pretty fast that if the cops are looking for you, it can't be for any reason you want to know. She's probably scared to death, hiding out in one of her holes. I thought I knew everywhere she'd go, but I can't even find her myself. She's got to be really shook up."

Seth said, "Say you're right and she's innocent. I'm still not sure what you want us to do. We're not private investigators."

Ace smiled slightly. "I wouldn't have any money to pay you if you were, but the two of you could still look around Vera's life and see who would want to do her harm. You two knew her, you traveled in some of the same circles so it wouldn't look suspicious if you asked a few questions."

Seth was thinking about the trip to the Florida Keys he and Gillian were taking the next day, an excursion they had planned for months. Friends of theirs owned a house on Big Pine Key, and they'd been after Seth and Gillian to visit them for years. On their limited incomes, it was the only way they could really afford to explore the Keys, and they'd both been looking forward to the trip. Seth was about to say something to Ace when Gillian read his eyes and spoke up, "We'll do what we can."

Seth raised an eyebrow and was rewarded with a slight shake of Gillian's head. Ace read this nearly imperceptible exchange and stood. "I can see you two have a lot to talk about, and I need to keep looking for Penny. I've got to find her before the police do."

Seth said, "If you do find her, you've got to convince her to go to the police. Otherwise it could be rough for you later if anything else turns up incriminating against her."

"I don't have a whole lot left to lose. I'm willing to take my chances."

After he was gone, Gillian came into Seth's arms. "I know we were going to visit Hank and Claire, but their house will be there whenever we're ready to go down."

"If a hurricane doesn't come through in the meantime. I'm still not sure what we can do."

"Seth, if we don't try, we'll never forgive ourselves." She tweaked him lightly on the cheek. "Besides, I can see you're considering the possibilities right now. You were too good a cop to let this slide. Admit it, a part of you thinks this is going to be fun."

"Murder's never fun, Gillian, I learned that a long time ago."

"Okay, a poor choice of words, I admit. Let's say you're

thinking about how satisfying it will be when we track down and expose the real murderer. You can't tell me it wouldn't be good to get back up on that horse one more time."

"I admit there are parts of my old job I miss, but there's one possibility I can't ignore. I live by Occam's Razor, the belief that the simplest explanation is probably the right one. If Penny did kill Vera, I don't want to have any part in putting her away. She's had enough troubles in her life, and I doubt she'd live to serve six months of a prison term or a stay in a mental institution."

Gillian stroked his shoulder lightly. "Wouldn't it be better to know for sure, one way or another? If she is capable of murder, she doesn't need to be on the street, and if she didn't do it, she doesn't deserve to be punished just because she's homeless."

"Okay, I'm convinced. You call Hank and Claire while I start making lists of the places we need to look and the people we need to see."

She kissed him deeply, then said, "You're a good man, Seth Jackson."

As he pulled her to him, he said, "Feel free to remind me just that way any time you like."

Seth began to explore the possibilities as Gillian left to make her telephone call. He'd been looking forward to spending some time away with her, shopping in Key West, doing a little snorkeling, swimming in the startling clear waters off the chain of islands. He'd wanted to see the Key deer living on Big Pine Key, wild animals in miniature who roamed the island at will. Hank had taken some beautiful photographs of the deer and shared them with him, but a photograph was a pale imitation of seeing the real thing for himself.

He took the pad and pen Gillian kept under her coffee table and tried to drag his thoughts back to the present task. Big Pine and the rest of the Florida Keys would still be there in another month; if he and Gillian were going to help Penny, he had to give it all of his concentration.

In the middle of the first sheet, Seth drew a circle and wrote 'Vera Hobart' inside. From this center, he began drawing radial lines outward for the people who touched her life. This wasn't a list of suspects particularly, just a rough sketch of who might know something about Vera's life, and more importantly, her death. The police would be focusing on Penny's involvement, and Seth would leave that to their more-than-capable hands. If her murder was indeed a random act of violence, it would be up to the Sheriff and his staff to discover that, too. Seth would have to concentrate on the circle of people surrounding the victim herself.

The first spoke he filled in was Bradley Hobart, the widower. Seth had run into Bradley a few times in the past, always at appreciation dinners given around town to the volunteers who regularly contributed their time and talent to the less fortunate. Seth wasn't a big fan of advertising the fact that he volunteered, it was a personal matter, and he liked to keep that way. Gillian, on the other hand, loved parties, dinners, any reason to style herself up above the everyday. The transformation was always startling to Seth. Gillian was lovely enough in her regular outfits, but there was nothing like a fancy dress to highlight her long slender legs, her graceful curves, and her regal cheekbones. It was almost worth attending the parties to see everyone else's reactions to Gillian's presence, a woman in her mid-forties who turned the heads of men from eighteen to eighty.

She certainly never failed to turn Bradley Hobart's head, though the man's roving eyes were by no means only for Gillian. Seth flipped the page and wrote Bradley's name in bold letters, then beneath it added, 'Having an affair? Jealous lover getting rid of competition? Vera insured? Check financial info. Did Bradley want a divorce? Ask around.'

He flipped back to another spoke and wrote in 'Jason Skyles'. Jason was Vera's son from her first marriage, and anyone who had ever worked with her on a volunteer project had heard the story of how her only child was back in her life again after a long absence. Seth knew Jason had a record, mostly for D&D, drunk and disorderly. From what Sheriff Kline had told him, the young man was a mean drunk, and no picnic to be around sober, either. Seth flipped back to the other page and wrote under Jason's name, 'Motive? Insurance? Could he have killed her in a drunken rage, some kind of Oedipal thing? Look into his whereabouts'.

Seth went back to the wheel and wrote Lex Bascum's name. On the list, he put down, 'Lex has volunteered a time or two, mostly for show. She's Vera's next door neighbor. Best friend? Any reason to be jealous of Vera, or want her dead? If not, could she know anything about someone who would? Talk to her soonest, she loves to gossip'.

Seth felt Gillian's arm reach across his shoulder as she tapped Lex's name. "If she knows anything, she'll tell us. That woman loves to talk."

Seth put the pad down. "What did Hank and Claire say?"

"They're disappointed, but they've got that Keys attitude of 'later'. Nothing seems to upset them too much. We've got an open invitation to visit whenever this mess is cleared up." She leaned forward and gave him a solid and very thorough kiss. After she broke away, she said, "That's from Claire."

Seth grinned. "I had no idea we'd grown that close."

"Neither does she. She said to kiss you for her, so I did."

"Remind me to thank her for that. I really can't wait to get down there now."

Gillian picked up the pad. "Consider it extra incentive to solve this case. What have you got so far?" She tapped Bradley's name. "He's a possibility, though I'm sure he thinks of himself as a lover, not a fighter. He's made several passes at me over the years, and he was smooth enough at it to make me think he's had lots of practice."

"Tell me about it," Seth said calmly.

Gillian looked at him carefully. "You're not going to get jealous, are you?"

Seth smiled. "Inside I'm a raging ball of fire, but I'm fighting to contain myself."

"You're doing a little too well, if you ask me."

"Gillian, I know he wouldn't stand a chance unless you were willing, and I happen to know you're not willing." Seth rubbed her shoulders gently, something he knew she loved. After a few moments, she said, "Okay, you're forgiven for not being more insanely jealous than you are. You'd better stop, you're putting me right to sleep."

"You say the most romantic things. Okay, I'll bite, did the blackguard try to corner you at a party, or pull you into a closet?"

"Nothing as overt as that. It's just the way he uses his eyes, the closeness of his stance, as if every move toward you is an invitation."

Seth nodded and underlined the words, 'Having an affair?', then said, "Anybody else you want to add to the list?"

"First we need to talk to Lex. I've got a hunch we'll be able to fill a notebook by the time she's done talking."

Seth frowned as he tapped the pencil in his hand. "There's just one thing wrong. What possible reason can we tell people we have for snooping around in Vera's life? I'm used to thinking like a cop, and the justification for asking questions was never a problem then."

"We don't need to say anything at all. People love to talk, and I've got a feeling all we need to do is act interested and we'll learn more than we expect."

Seth dropped the pencil on the table. "Okay, we'll give it a try." He stood, then reached down to pull Gillian to her feet. "Let's go talk to Lex and see if she can add anything to our list."

Chapter 4

Gillian would never admit it to anyone, especially Seth, but most days she preferred riding around in his old Ford pickup truck than her own sporty little Subaru. There was something about being up in the truck's cab well above her usual perspective that gave Gillian a feeling of power. Too, the truck had taken more than its share of casual abuse on the Christmas Tree farm, so Seth never worried about additional scratches or the possibility of an accident marring its finish.

Lex's house was easy to find; it was at the entrance of Jackson's Ferry's only gated community, Jackson's Ferry. Seth didn't even slow down as the gray-uniformed guard approached. The guard could only offer a stern wave of his hand as the truck slid casually through the narrow slice of road unimpeded.

Gillian asked, "Why do they have a guard and a gate if the guy's not going to do anything to keep anybody out?"

Seth laughed. "Don't blame him, it's not his fault. Jackson's Ferry wants to give the world the impression that they're some kind of exclusive development, but they're not willing to absorb the cost of maintaining their own roads within the property. The law says that no state maintained road can be gated, but they've tried their best to intimidate people coming in, anyway."

"They just didn't count on running into a criminal justice professor who also happened to be an ex-cop."

"Don't kid yourself, Gillian. With this truck, the guy probably just figured I was with one of the trades doing work around the development."

Seth pulled up into Lex Bascum's driveway. Gillian had gotten the address from the telephone book. It was a two-story brick Colonial sporting two white columns holding up a small portico. The lawn needed to be mowed, but Gillian doubted anyone in Jackson's Ferry would actually trim their own grass. What the neighbors thought carried more weight than simple economics. It was a trap Gillian had been in herself at one point in her life, always trying to keep up with everyone else, normally through overextending limited resources. Though her income as a full time stockbroker had been handsome, equal to and sometimes exceeding her husband's as a fellow stockbroker, they'd still managed to be in debt to a half dozen financial institutions at any one time. When the marriage had died from lack of interest on both their parts just before her father's long bout with cancer, it had been almost a relief in one way; Gillian managed to pay off her share of the marital debt, working long hours so she wouldn't have to go home alone to her empty apartment. Her father's death had only reinforced what she'd painfully learned on her own again; the quest for more 'things' could take the life out of life. After the funeral, she'd scaled back her clientele to just one; she managed the portfolio of the Larkin Foundation, a group set up for the distribution of its accrued interest to worthy charities in the state of North Carolina. Under Gillian's gifted touch, the foundation's portfolio had grown in size nearly every quarter. It provided enough income to for her to live on, and allowed her the time she needed to enjoy her life. Finding Seth had been a direct link to her lifestyle choice; they'd met on a Habitat for Humanity house building site, and an immediate chemistry had flared between them. By the time the house was finished three months later, the two of them had become intrinsic parts of each other's lives.

 Seth leaned on the bell for the third time, but there was still no response from inside the house.

 Gillian said, "It doesn't look like anybody's home."

 "We're not giving up that easily." They walked back to the side entrance garage, and Seth peeked through one of the door's windows. He banged loudly on the glass, and Gillian was afraid it would shatter under his assault. A few seconds later the side door opened. Lex Bascom had a pair of earphones around her neck, and even from where she stood

Gillian could hear the music cascading out. In her mid thirties, Lex was dressed casually, her hair mostly hidden by a blue paisley bandanna. There were smudges of dirt on her face, and Gillian could see that Lex's hands were soiled as well. The oversized baggy sweatshirt and jeans couldn't fully disguise the fact that Lex was at least twenty pounds overweight, and Gillian couldn't remember ever seeing her that heavy. She obviously still retained a lot of the strength she'd acquired working out at the gym; some of those boxes she'd been moving around were huge. From the redness in her eyes, Gillian could see that she'd been crying. There was obvious pain in Lex's eyes, and Gillian's instinct was to wrap her arms around the woman and give her a hug. They weren't there to offer comfort though, so Gillian remained beside Seth.

She was certain Seth picked up the same indicators she had. He was the most perceptive, empathetic man she'd ever known, but there was none of that in his voice as he said, "Sorry to bother you." He'd unconsciously gone into his police mode, interrogating a witness.

Lex shut off the portable stereo and pulled the earphones from around her neck. There was an air of sadness in her voice as she said, "I was ready for a break anyway. What can I do for you two?"

Seth glanced at Gillian. She could see an 'I told you this wasn't going to work' in his eyes, something that made her more determined than ever to prove that she had the right idea about what their approach should be.

Gently, Gillian said, "Have you heard the news yet? Vera's dead."

Lex nodded. "It was just on the radio."

"We were at the soup kitchen today working when she stumbled in and died. It was just awful."

Lex nodded with a grim line to her lips. "I told Vera a thousand times that place was too dangerous, but would she listen to me?" Suddenly backpedaling, obviously realizing her audience, Lex added, "I think what you'all do is wonderful, but it's not without its risks, you've got to admit that. I finally had to give it up myself, no matter how much I enjoyed helping others less fortunate."

Gillian was about to defend her lifestyle choice when she felt Seth's eyes on her. The cop in him was in full charge, letting the witness speak without interruption.

When Lex saw that there'd be no protest, she continued. "Would you'all like some tea? I'm doing some real grunt work in here, and I could use a cold glass myself."

Seth nodded, and the three of them went inside the garage. There was a mountain of new boxes there, some not even folded together yet, along with a card table obviously set up as a packing station. The table was heaped with women's clothes that had gone out of style years ago. It appeared that Lex was one of those women who hated to get rid of anything she'd ever worn. Gillian asked, "You're not moving, are you, Lex?"

"Don't even get me started about that." There was a harshness in her voice that told Gillian to drop the subject, especially if she expected to get anything useful out of Lex.

They took the offered tea, and Gillian found it too sweet for her tastes. Though the South was famous for its iced tea, the quality varied. Seth gulped his down, asking for a refill almost immediately. Gillian knew he was a sugar addict, one reason he was unable to take off the extra pounds he carried around.

After taking a healthy swallow of the refill, Seth said, "You were Vera's best friend, weren't you? You must really be shaken up by all of this."

They sat in an intimate little breakfast nook just off the kitchen that offered a view of the woods that surrounded the development. Though a screen of oak and maple saplings outlined the edge of the property itself, towering over the new trees was a massive stand of scrub pine, a testament to what had covered the land before the developers had arrived.

Lex said, "It's been one monster of a week." After a deep breath, she added, "I might as well tell you, you'll hear it soon enough. That rat husband of mine is leaving me for his little chippie secretary. That's why I'm loading boxes; I refuse to stay in this house a minute longer than I have to. He can have it all, as far as I'm concerned, I just want what I came into the marriage with."

Gillian saw the blaze in Lex's eyes, and felt the underlying pain of the betrayal. That explained the almost haunted look in Lex's eyes she'd seen. The woman really had been put through the mill. She doubted they'd be getting anything useful out of her, but Seth spoke before Gillian had a chance to say anything about leaving.

"Would you like to talk about Vera? It might help, talking out loud about it with people who care."

Lex reached out and touched Seth's hand lightly. "Thanks, that would be nice." Lex went on. "Vera cared too much, that was her main problem in life. If there was anything in the world she saw needed fixing, she'd jump right in with both feet. I don't have to tell you two that, though do I? You're both like that, too."

Gillian asked, "As Vera's best friend, who else was she friends with?"

"I don't think you could say we were best friends. You'd be surprised, but Vera didn't have all that many friends. She had a way of driving people off with her attitudes." Lex thought a moment, then added, "That's not very charitable, is it? We're only supposed to speak well of the dead. Poor Vera isn't around to defend herself anymore."

Seth stepped in lightly. "Anybody in particular she alienated?"

Lex swirled the tea in her glass before speaking. "If you had the time, I could make a list. Half the neighbors on the block, for starters. Vera was our self-appointed moral guardian in the development, and she wasn't afraid to tell people what she thought." Gillian knew that to be true of her own contact with Vera. The woman had lectured them both on the moral high-ground of marriage over sin at least a dozen times. Gillian had been angry with the woman's intrusiveness, but Seth had always managed to defuse the situation by teasing Vera out of her stern moods. He had a way of disarming people with things said humorously, comments that, if stated plainly, would set them boiling.

The door bell chimed, and Lex excused herself. Gillian said quietly, "She's not much help, is she?"

Seth put a finger to his lips as he stood. "Let's see who's visiting."

As they approached the door, they saw Lex in animated conversation with the United Parcel Service delivery man. She was waving an Overnight Express envelope in his face. "I'm not taking this, do you hear me? If I'd known it was from him, I'd never have signed for it."

As the man beat a hasty retreat back to the security of his brown van, he called out, "Ma'am, there's nothing I can do about it."

She threw the envelope into the yard. "I'm not accepting it, do you hear me?"

As he pulled down the driveway, he said, "I'm sorry, Ma'am. I'm just doing my job." There was a look of pure relief on his face as he drove away.

Lex watched him in anger, then retrieved the delivered envelope. Seth and Gillian quickly walked back to the table where they'd been sitting.

Lex said, "Sorry, this day just keeps getting worse."

"We won't keep you from your work," Gillian said. As they made their way back out through the garage, she looked back toward their host. Instead of looking at them, Lex was staring at the envelope. Gillian wondered if she was searching for the courage to open it.

Once they were out of Lex's hearing, Seth said, "She wasn't done talking to us. When people are the most upset, a lot of times that's when you find out the truth of what's really going on."

"She was in pain, Seth. I just couldn't force myself to take advantage of it."

He touched Gillian lightly. "I know, but if you're going

to investigate with me, you're going to have to learn to put your personal feelings aside. You've got a good heart, Gillian, but you can't let it get in the way."

She nodded soberly. Investigating Vera's death would take a change in her attitude, but it was one she was willing to make. If it meant people around Jackson's Ferry thought she'd suddenly become a shrew, it was worth it to save Penny.

Before they could get into the truck, Gillian took a deep breath and said, "Why don't we go see if the widower's home?"

"Aren't you the woman who just stopped interrogating a witness because she was feeling blue? Are you certain you want to tackle a fresh, grieving husband?"

Gillian shrugged. "You've convinced me that we're going to have to step on some toes if we're going to uncover the truth." She paused a second, then added, "Besides, we need to know if he's really grieving."

Seth looked at her for a second, studying her, then nodded his assent. "It's a great idea. Let's do it."

As she led the way across a strip of grass that separated the two driveways, Gillian wondered just how much Bradley Hobart had loved his wife. The man had certainly spent enough of his time trying to get into her own panties. Her rebuffs at parties and social events that threw them together had begun as gentle refusals that had quickly escalated into rude, abrupt comments and threats of violence. Ordinarily, Gillian had no trouble making her intentions understood. At a notch over six feet, she could be a dominating presence, and a curt word or two along with her iciest glare normally deterred even the most ardent suitor. But with Bradley, nothing had worked. The man actually believed there was some attraction all women had to him, and his mission in life was not to deny them his pleasures. Personally, he disgusted Gillian. She wondered if he'd try to make a pass at her the day his wife was murdered. She wouldn't put it past him. Gillian had avoided mentioning the severity of his behavior to Seth for a number of reasons. First, while it was true he was persistent, he'd never actually tried to touch her in any way; Hobart probably knew she'd break his arm if he did. Second, there was something in her that hated to admit to Seth or anyone else that there was a situation she couldn't handle herself. Last, Gillian was afraid of what Seth might do if he actually knew the extent of Hobart's passes. Outwardly, Seth presented a 'teddy bear' quality to the world, but she'd seen the steel of his rage a time or two and knew it was a force to be reckoned with. All things considered, Bradley Hobart wasn't worth an assault charge against Seth, and most likely something worse.

Seth started to ring the bell when he motioned to Gillian that the front door was ajar. Easing himself to the gap, he lifted a finger to his lips. Gillian moved closer, and could hear Hobart's unmistakable voice. It was obvious by the gaps in his conversation that he was speaking with someone on the telephone, someone he was having an argument with.

"No, you can't come over here. I don't want to see you at the funeral, either. Why? My God, you're really dense, aren't you?" His voice grew louder, as if he were pacing around the house. "What? You've got to be kidding. I'm telling you--." An abrupt break, then a near whisper, "I've got to go."

Seth took that moment to ring the doorbell, but it was obvious Hobart had already seen them. He flung the door open and said, "What do you two want?"

Bradley Hobart was in his early forties, right around Seth's age, but the two men couldn't have been more different. While Seth was comfortable with his age, Hobart was obviously fighting the battle against growing older with every ounce of energy he had. Hobart's hair, though thinning, touched his shoulders in back.

"We came by to offer our condolences. Is there anything we can do to help?"

"No, I just want to be alone right now."

Hobart moved aside reluctantly and they walked inside

the house. Gillian quickly looked to find the closest portable telephone.

Seth said, "Surely you shouldn't be by yourself at a time like this."

A bit impatiently, Hobart said, "My brother's coming in from Boone, he should be here any minute. Now if you two will excuse me, I've got some things I need to take care of."

Gillian caught Seth's eye and made a quick motion she was sure Hobart couldn't see. As the widower was trying to ease them out the door, Seth said, "I hate to bother you, but I've got a tickle in my throat that's driving me crazy. Could I get a quick drink of water? It'll only take a minute."

Hobart looked as if he wanted to deny the request, then shrugged. "Okay, come on, the kitchen's through here."

As Seth followed Hobart out of the room, he raised an eyebrow to Gillian, who urged him on with her eyes. The second they were gone, Gillian took the telephone from its hook, turned it on, and hit the redial button. After a single ring, she heard a woman's voice say breathlessly, "Hello?"

Gillian knew that voice, but she couldn't instantly place it. She heard, "Hello," one more time, and then an abrupt disconnect. At that moment, Hobart came back into the room. "I thought you were coming with us. What are you doing with my phone?"

Hanging it back up in its cradle, Gillian said, "I had to check my messages, I'm expecting a call. I didn't think you'd mind."

The cloud passed quickly from his face as he advanced toward her. She couldn't believe it; the son of a dog was actually going to make a pass at her. He was two steps from her, a greasy smile pasted to his face, when Seth said, "Thanks, that water took care of the tickle."

Hobart's smile disappeared in an instant. "No problem," he said, a comment he obviously didn't mean. As he held the door open for them, he said insincerely, "Thanks for stopping by. Now if you'll excuse me, I've got to get things ready for the service tomorrow afternoon."

Gillian said, "So soon?"

"It was Vera's wish. She always said she wanted to be cremated as soon as possible after she died, she had some morbid fears about her body lying around after she was gone. The cremation's scheduled for tonight."

Seth looked surprised. "The police have already released the body to you?"

Hobart snapped, "And why shouldn't they? Some bum stuck a knife in her ribs. One of the policemen who came by told me they had a pretty good idea who did it and why."

This was news to them. Seth asked, "Why? She had all of her money on her, from what I heard."

"Haven't you heard? Her diamond engagement ring was gone, and she'd never have taken it off willingly. It was worth a lot more than the petty cash she carried around with her whenever she went to volunteer. When I told the police about its absence as I picked up Vera's things, they seemed to be pretty happy about."

Inwardly, Gillian groaned. If it was the truth, the ring's absence was one more strike against Penny. Even if it didn't turn up after she was found, the police could always claim she'd already sold it, or gotten rid of it somehow. It added a motive to the crime, something that wouldn't fare well for her.

When Seth and Gillian walked back to their truck, still parked in Lex's driveway, they found Lex leaning against the tailgate. From the look on her face, it was obvious the woman had something else to say to them.

Chapter 5

As a cop, Seth had developed a sixth sense with witnesses, whether it was by reading their body language or picking up other signs subconsciously, but for whatever the reason, there was no doubt in his mind Lex had decided to unburden herself. He glanced at Gillian and whispered, "Let me handle this." He didn't want any sympathy on her part to defuse Lex's determination.

Seth muttered a curt, "Lex," as they approached. The less he said at this point, the better.

"So, how's Bradley taking the news?"

He could smell liquor on her breath. She'd evidently decided that alcohol could help. Good, maybe it would loosen her tongue. "He seems to be holding up."

Lex laughed callously. "I'm sure he's doing just fine. Did he tell you the truth?"

Gently, Seth asked, "Which truth is that, Lex?"

"The truth about his marriage, or the lack of it. I'll bet even money he's in there pretending to mourn Vera's death, but let me tell you something, that's all it is, an act."

Gillian matched Seth's tone as she said, "What do you mean?" Seth was pleased she'd picked up on his questioning technique so quickly. Some of the questions they needed to ask would sound a great deal better coming from another woman.

"He's got you fooled, too, doesn't he," she snapped out.

Gillian shook her head softly. "All we want to hear is the truth."

Lex took a step closer to them and said, "You asked for it, so here goes." She nodded toward the Hobart house next door. "It looks like a slice of suburban heaven, but don't trust your eyes. Vera told me good old Bradley's been asking for a divorce for the past six weeks; asking; it was more like demanding. Vera laughed it off, she said it was a phase he was going through, some kind of mid-life crisis. That made him even madder, from what she told me. The more times she refused him, the angrier he got. I think she was beginning to be afraid of him, if you want the truth of it."

Gillian said, "Bradley didn't need her permission to get a divorce."

Lex jerked her head, as if she'd been focusing on something else. "He did if he wanted to keep his precious reputation intact. Vera told me she'd fight him tooth and nail if he pursued it, and a messy divorce would mean Bradley the Great had failed at something; he wasn't about to admit that to the world." She paused to shoot a look of hatred in the direction of the house next door, then added, "I guess Bradley won't have to go the trouble of filing for divorce now. It's a sight better to be widowed than divorced, so I guess he got his way after all, didn't he?"

Seth studied Lex as she spoke. There was no doubt she'd been drinking, but had the amount of alcohol in her system been just enough to get her courage up, or was every supposed fact she was sharing with them straight out of the bottle?

He said, "Was there another woman involved?"

"Singular?" Lex snapped. "Not on your life. In case you hadn't noticed, good old Bradley's got a bad habit, he can't leave women alone." She gave Gillian a knowing look. "But I don't have to tell you that, do I, sweetie? I've seen him after you at parties. Did he ever get you?"

"Only in his dreams."

Lex laughed harshly. "Good for you. I'll say this for the guy, he's persistent enough when he sees something, or should I say someone he wants."

Gillian avoided Seth's glance, a sure sign that she was hiding something herself. After they were through with Lex, he was going to have to get the facts about the extent of Bradley Hobart's advances.

Gillian added, more for Seth's benefit than Lex's, "He

made a few passes, but he never laid a finger on me."

Lex looked at her with disbelief. "Then you're the first woman he went after who found a way to turn him down."

Seth probed. "Does that include you?"

"Me, sleep with him? Not only was Vera my friend, but I wouldn't have touched Bradley Hobart on a bet, even if he were single. Snakes and wolves I can do without, thank you very much."

"Do you have any idea who he was sleeping with lately?"

Lex looked angry as she said, "Make a list of the women in Jackson's Ferry, and I'm sure you'll have a pretty good idea. Good old Bradley's an equal opportunity sleaze bag, he didn't discriminate in any way." She rubbed her forehead with her hand, then said, "Lately? That's a little harder to say. I'd look pretty close near his office in town, if I had to make a guess. Whenever Vera was away from the house on a fund-raiser, he always worked late, or so he told her."

Inside, the shrill ring of the telephone carried outside. "Excuse me, I'm expecting a call. It's going to be a long one, so there's no need to wait." As she closed the door, Lex said, "See you at the wake. It should be one whale of a show."

Seth and Gillian got into the truck and backed out of the driveway. "What now?" Gillian asked.

"I'd like to find out if half of what Lex told us is true. If she's not lying, Hobart had a real reason to want Vera dead. From the sound of it, Vera had reason of her own to wish her husband ill. Add that to Lex's divorce and her own husband's philandering, and it sounds like another day in paradise."

"I don't envy her, divorce can be a nasty thing."

"At least she's got the option of moving on, that's more than Vera got."

Gillian nodded. "Who should we interview next?"

"I'd like to talk to Vera's son Jason and see if she said anything to him about the divorce."

"You know him very well?"

Seth shrugged. "He's done some welding for me around the farm in the past. He hates to do anything practical, though, he thinks of himself solely as a sculptor, a real artiste. He's pretty good, too. Jason is a tough nut to read, one day he's your best friend in the world, and the next he acts as if he doesn't know you. Another thing, he's got one of the worst tempers I've ever seen, and that's saying something. He's got a record for being drunk and disorderly, but Skyles can be just as nasty without a drop of alcohol in him."

"He sounds like a real charming fellow." After a few moments of silence, Gillian added, "Seth, you really don't think Penny could have killed Vera, do you?"

As he turned the corner and headed out in the country toward Jason Skyles' place, he said, "She's a possibility, I won't lie to you. For argument's sake, let's say she didn't kill Vera. Maybe she knows a little more about what happened to her knife than she told Ace. She might have even seen something she shouldn't have. However you cut it, I'd feel a lot better if we knew where she was."

Gillian picked up on the tone of his voice. "Do you think something's happened to her?"

He shrugged. "If she saw something, it's a possibility that the murderer wanted to get rid of a witness." Seth saw that Gillian was worried, and though she presented a solid, unflappable guise to the world, he knew a softer side of her. As he patted her hand lightly, he said, "Gillian, we're going to do our best to uncover the truth. It's going to hurt some people, you can bet on that, but it's still a worthy goal."

"Guilty or innocent all the way, is that it?"

He shook his head sadly. Though she'd been the daughter of a cop and had learned a great many of her dad's attitudes and ways of looking at things, Gillian had never been hardened by the ugly streets Seth had experienced. "I've always been willing to leave guilt or innocence to the court system. All I want to find is the truth; let the lawyers sort out the burden of blame, I'm not interested."

"Isn't the truth and justice one and the same?"

Seth said, "You couldn't prove it by me."

"So cynical for one so young."

Seth picked up on her attempt to lighten the mood of their conversation, but there was still one more point he needed to clear up. "I like to think of myself as a realist. We need to talk about Bradley Hobart."

"He's a real prince, isn't he?"

Seth gripped the wheel tightly, keeping his eyes on the road. His next question was going to have to be worded delicately. "Did anything ever happen between the two of you we need to talk about?"

"Nothing."

Seth took a deep breath. "Gillian, I know he was after you, any man in his right mind who still has a pulse would be. I just need to know if it went any further than a pass."

"He never touched me, Seth, no matter how overt his advances were. I swear it."

Seth pulled his truck into Jason's long gravel driveway and said, "That's good enough for me." Seth hated tension between them, but it was a question he had to ask.

After a moment's silence between them, she said, "Seth, do you trust me?"

He stopped the truck, took her into his arms and gave her a reassuring hug. "With my life."

Their tension melted in the aura of their embrace. After a few seconds, she pulled away and said, "I trust you, too." Then with an impish grin, she added, "Just not with Nurse Nancy. I know you can be jealous, but I can, too. You get any cuts or bruises, you come to me."

He laughed gladly. "That's a promise."

Gillian toyed with a ring on her finger, then asked, "What do you think really happened to Vera's ring? Was Bradley lying about it to give Penny a motive?"

"The ring wasn't on her finger when she came in the door, I can swear to that much."

Gillian looked surprised. "How can you be so sure?"

"Years of training. I don't mean to size people up the instant I see them, it's just an old habit I can't seem to break. Vera wasn't wearing her wedding ring when she came into the soup kitchen."

"So where did it go?"

"I can see a few possibilities, but Bradley's right, that was the first time in all of the years I've known Vera that I've seen her without it. If she and Bradley were splitting up, maybe she took it off in disgust. She could have sold it, for all we know. I just hope to God it doesn't show up somewhere else."

Gillian nodded. "Like on Penny's finger, I know, I was just thinking the same thing."

"I had three different partners while I was on the force, and I swear none of them had a thing on you."

She kissed him lightly on the cheek. "Thank you, kind sir. Now, are we going to sit here all day, or are we going to see if Jason Skyles knew anything about his mother's divorce?"

"Are you sure you want to go with me? Maybe it's not such a great idea you being here. Like I said, the man's got a brutal disposition, and I have no idea how he's reacting to his mother's death."

Gillian gave his arm a squeeze. "We're partners, remember?"

"I know, but we can be partners from a distance. Can I drive you out to my house and come back for you later?"

"Seth, I'm going where you're going. We're investigating a murder, and I'm not about to let you take all the chances yourself. Besides, maybe Jason will mind his manners if I'm around. I've been known to have that effect on men."

Seth nodded unhappily, refusing to rise to her jibe. "Just take your cues from me. When I make a move to leave, don't hesitate."

"I promise."

As they drove the remaining forty yards to Jason Skyles'

studio-barn and house, Seth silently regretted not coming out alone. He knew Gillian was a full grown woman able to take care of herself, but he still felt responsible for her safety. He suddenly found himself hoping that Jason Skyles hadn't started hitting the bottle yet; he was tough enough to deal with sober.

The house and barn where Jason worked and lived had seen better days, most likely in the nineteen forties. Weeds grew up to the house's front steps; there were even a few vigorous weeds growing in the gutters, a sure sign that Jason hadn't bothered cleaning them for years. The clapboards of the small frame house were a faded shade of beige, the color of vanilla ice cream left out in the rain, and it was hard to say what the original color of the barn had been. Both structures were desperate for a coat of paint and a thousand little things it took to keep a building sound.

Skyles must have heard them as they drove up. Before they could get out of the truck, he was approaching from the barn. Tall and lanky, he wore the heavy leather gloves, thick apron and dark tinted mask of his welder's trade. Beneath the equipment, Jason wore black, from his boots to his jeans to his shirt. Seth knew it wasn't a basic mourning outfit; Skyles liked to consider himself an artiste, and he always dressed the part. In one gloved hand was a chunk of hardened steel the size of a billy club, and from the way the welder held it, it looked more like a potential weapon than a piece of work. The visor flipped up, and Jason's cold gray eyes studied Seth for a moment before taking a more leisurely approach to Gillian. There wasn't a hint of grief in the eyes, and Seth wondered if the man even knew his mother was dead. It was always the part of being a cop that Seth had hated most, telling someone that a loved one was gone, forever.

As Seth tried to find the right words, Skyles said, "I already know, Vera's dead." There wasn't a touch of softness in his voice as he used her given name instead of a more familiar acknowledgment that the victim had been his mother.

    Seth nodded. "We just wanted to come by and offer our condolences."

    Skyles took off the visor, tucked the hunk of steel under one arm, then removed the heavy glove on his right hand. He took a step forward and offered his bare hand to Gillian. "We haven't met, I'm Jason Skyles."

    Gillian took his hand. "Gillian Goldhawk."

    Skyles studied her a moment before releasing her hand. "I'd love to sculpt you, you have beautiful bones. Any chance of you posing for me?"

    Gillian laughed gently as she pulled her hand away. "I'm an art lover, not a model."

    Skyles shrugged. "You change your mind, let me know. Anytime, day or night."

    "You're taking your mother's death well," Seth said. He hadn't expected tears, but he thought Skyles would at least be too upset to make a pass at Gillian, in front of him no less. He hadn't thought of the man as a wolf, but maybe Gillian's presence was all it took to bring that side out.

    Skyles said, "We each grieve in our own way. I choose to lose myself in my work. Have they found that bag lady who killed her yet?"

    "Nobody's sure she did it, Jason."

    "Come on, Seth, you were a cop. It was her knife, for God's sake, and from what Bradley tells me, Vera's ring is gone. My asshole stepfather seemed more upset about the diamond being stolen than Vera's death. I hope the police are looking at his alibi, too."

    Gillian asked, "Didn't they get along?"

    "Sure, as long as Vera ignored the jerk's affairs and kept her mouth shut. I told her a thousand times to get out, but she wouldn't listen to me. She kept defending him, telling the world that Bradley was an open flirt, but that he never did anything more than that. Trust me, he did a whale of a lot more than just flirt."

    "Anybody in particular?" Gillian asked.

"No, I don't think he was that particular at all." Skyles slipped a hand back into his glove, then said, "Thanks for coming by. I've got to get back to my work."

Seth wasn't ready to finish the interview, but the abrupt dismissal in Skyles' voice was obvious.

Seth felt Gillian reading him, something she'd grown quite adept at in the time they'd been together. She said, "I'd really like to see what you do. Could we have a look?"

He shook his head. "Sorry, no tours around here. I'm not fond of people looking over my shoulder while I'm working." His tone had grown definitely chilled.

Gillian appeared to ignore it. "Now how am I supposed to decide if I want to pose or not if I can't look at what you've done."

Skyles looked at her body again, and Seth felt his temper starting to edge upward. He was about to tell the welder to forget it when the man nodded. "You've got a point. Come on in. But I'm warning you, you can only stay a minute."

Gillian nodded and followed Skyles in through the barn's side door. As she stepped through, she turned back to Seth and offered a broad wink. Seth grinned back at her. He had to admit it, having her along had turned into an asset. He'd never seen Skyles so polite. He wondered briefly if his mother's death had shaken him more than he wanted to show, or if he was serious about Gillian posing nude for him. He didn't think there was a chance of that really happening, but with Gillian, he'd almost grown to expect the unexpected. She was the strongest woman he'd ever known, seemingly having a sixth sense about what was right for her, and what was not.

The interior of the barn was nothing like its exterior. The central space was clean and well lit. There was a working area with vises, benches and an arc welder, while surrounding it were racks of metal, round rods, flat rods and random pieces of jetsam that appeared to be hundreds of years old. On the central stand now was a graceful figure of a pregnant woman in black steel, her hands on her distended belly. Seth had to admit the sculpture was excellent. Skyles was watching their reaction, and what he saw must have pleased him. He explained, "It's for Dr. Larkin. I figure she's in OB/GYN, so she might like this."

Gillian said, "It's beautiful. Can I see more of your work?"

He nodded, and Seth could see the beginnings of a smile on the man's face. He never would have believed Jason Skyles even knew how to. Gillian was truly something.

Skyles pointed to a mirror leaning against a wall, gently woven round rods of steel twisted into an ivy frame with delicate leaves and grasping tendrils. The piece almost looked alive. Gillian was truly taken with it, Seth could see it in her eyes. He wished he could buy it for her, but there was no way on his income he could afford it. That was the only problem with his lifestyle choice, one he rarely regretted. Seth brought in enough money from the farm to dine at nice restaurants and even take a trip now and then, but he wasn't in any position to make large purchases. Still, it was a small price to pay to live the life he'd chosen for himself after his wife's death.

Trying to divert Gillian's attention from the mirror, Seth asked Skyles, "Have you been here working all day?"

The man nodded, then suddenly his eyes narrowed. "You asking me if I have an alibi, Seth? You think I could have had something to do with killing my own mother?"

"Take it easy, I was just wondering."

The welder's previously good mood was gone. "Yeah, once a cop always a cop. I need to get back to work if I'm going to deliver this on time. You two need to go."

He was about to protest when Skyles flipped his visor back down and fired up the welder. Seth knew the bright light could damage their eyes, so he ushered Gillian out quickly.

Seth said, "Sorry about that. I had to ask, but I'm beginning to think I should have left the questioning to you."

"He would have reacted the same way to me. What do

you think?"

"I doubt we'll get anything else from him today."

As they got into the truck, Gillian asked, "Do you really think someone that talented could kill his own mother?"

"Come on, just because he's good with metal doesn't mean he's an angel in the rest of his life. I've seen him in action, he can be a real brute."

Gillian nodded. "I know, you said that before, but it's hard to imagine."

"That mirror caught your eye, didn't it? Do you ever regret giving up the bulk of your career, not to mention all of that money coming in?"

"Not for a second. That life wasn't living, it was just getting by from deal to deal. For the first time in my life, I'm living, instead of just letting things happen."

She kissed him gently on the cheek. "Besides, I'd have never met you."

"Good answer," Seth said as he turned the truck around and headed back toward town.

Gillian laughed gently. "I knew you'd like it." They rode in silence a few minutes, then she asked, "What time is it, Seth?"

"Nearly seven, why?"

"I don't know about you, but I'm getting hungry. It's been a long time since we ate at the soup kitchen at eleven. Why don't we go to Louie's and see if our corner booth is available. It would be nice to have a quiet meal and discuss everything we've seen and heard today over a glass of wine."

"That sounds good, but there's one place I'd like to stop before we eat."

Gillian said, "Let me guess, it's got to be the police station or the homeless shelter. You want to know if anybody's found Penny yet, don't you?"

As he swerved the truck to avoid a suicidal squirrel trying to streak across the road, he said, "The police station it is. I've got to admit, the cop in me is wondering if we've been spinning our wheels today. If the sheriff can prove that

Penny killed Vera, we're making enemies fast for no good reason."

"I didn't think you cared if people liked you or not."

"Gillian, what we're doing is intrusive, no matter what front we put on it. I'd feel better about it if we could talk to Penny ourselves."

After pulling up in front of the station, he asked, "You coming in?"

"No, I think I'll wait out here. You'll probably get more out of them if I'm not there. Besides, I want to walk over to my loft and take a quick shower." She arched an eyebrow and said, "If you hurry, you can scrub my back."

Seth kissed her lightly. "I've suddenly got new incentive to make things quick, don't I?"

"That's what I'm counting on."

Seth asked the cop on duty at the front desk, a man he knew slightly, if Sheriff Kline was in.

The cop nodded, then said softly, "I'd take it easy if I were you, he's in a ripper of a mood."

"Thanks, appreciate the advice."

Kline must have heard them talking. He came out into the lobby and said, "I thought you were retired. What are you doing hanging around?"

"I was just wondering if you'd found Penny yet."

The sheriff said coolly, "What's your interest in this, Seth?"

He shrugged. "Think of me as a concerned citizen."

"Yeah, right. I don't want you messing around with this one, you hear me? I'm the sheriff."

Seth tried to smile, though he didn't feel much like it. "I understand. Like I said, I just want to know if she's been found."

Sheriff Kline looked at him a second, then said, "I don't guess it'll hurt to tell you. She's still missing, but I expect to find her any minute. There can't be that many places to hide downtown."

"Do me a favor, let me know when she turns up, will you?"

Kline said darkly, "Professional courtesy?"

"Let's just say as a favor to me."

Kline nodded. "If I can remember, I will. Now get out of here so I can get to work."

Seth nodded. "I'm already gone, there's someplace else I need to be."

As he hurriedly drove to Gillian's loft, he empathized with the sheriff. Vera's death was high profile, and the mayor and town council would be on his back until he found the killer. Seth was sure they'd been after him to bring in the State Bureau of Investigation boys to help, but knowing the sheriff, he'd crawl through broken glass before he asked an outsider for help. Ace's concerns that Penny would be railroaded into an arrest weren't unfounded, not that Seth would blame the sheriff. In nine cases out of ten, the most obvious answer was the correct one, enough of a track record to give cops a healthy respect for looking hard at the most likely suspect.

Still, there was a distinct possibility that this case was that one in ten where the simplest explanation wasn't necessarily the best one. He was determined to find the truth, no matter how many toes he had to step on to uncover it. The sheriff was a good cop and a fair man; if Seth and Gillian discovered any pertinent facts in the case, he'd give them a fair hearing. So far, though, all they had were impressions and guesses, not anything as substantial as a real piece of evidence.

When he got to Gillian's he was disappointed to hear that the shower wasn't running.

She came out of the bathroom smiling, wearing only a bra and panties. "My back could really use a scrubbing, so I waited for you. We can take our time in the shower, our dinner reservation's not for another hour."

As Seth started taking off his clothes, he smiled at her. "Sometimes, life can be very good."

Chapter 6

As she sat across the table from Seth at Louie's, one of their favorite restaurants in Jackson's Ferry, Gillian could see something in her companion's eyes that troubled her. It was a stirring, an uneasiness that she recognized immediately, almost as if he were being haunted by internal ghosts. Gillian doubted it had anything to do with the case, at least not directly. She'd seen that expression before, and never really knew how to handle it. Reaching across the tablecloth and touching his hand, she said, "Do you want to talk about it?"

"The case? No, right now all I want to do is concentrate on my food. Where is it, anyway? It's just a steak, for God's sake."

She added a little pressure to her touch. "I'm not talking about Vera and you know it. You've been thinking about Melissa again, haven't you?" Seth's dead wife was the one subject in his life that he refused to discuss with her. Gillian wished he'd open up to her about that part of his past life, but she'd learned early on not to mention it unless she felt compelled by his black moods. He'd awakened more than once in her bed in the middle of the night, shaking in a cold sweat calling Melissa's name. Gillian had tried everything she knew, from patience to gentle probing, but the result was always the same: silence.

Seth shrugged as he pulled his hand away from hers. "It's nothing. Hey, here's our food. I'm starving." The dismissal in his voice was firm, so Gillian accepted his blatantly false statement. She had to believe when the time was right, he'd tell her. She just wished he'd open up and share that last part of himself with her.

Seth looked at the grilled vegetables on her plate with a crinkled nose and said, "Don't you ever get tired of eating that rabbit food? I'd be happy to share some of my steak with you."

Gillian lowered her chin and said lightly, "Hey, you want to eat something that loved its mother, that's your business." It was a long-standing discussion between them, one of many issues in their lives they'd agreed to disagree about.

Seth smiled as he cut into the meat. "It's a sacrifice I'm willing to accept." The trouble in his eyes disappeared as he ate, obviously relishing every bite.

Gillian watched him for a moment. "You really enjoy eating that, don't you?"

Seth laughed. "Would it make you feel better if I felt guilty about it?"

"Sometimes I have a hard time understanding how someone so caring about people could eat meat, let alone be a diehard conservative like you are."

Seth took a sip of red wine, then said, "Certainly I care about people, I just don't extend the innate sanctity of life to cattle or chickens or pigs. I'm not about to apologize to anyone for what I like to eat. The animals that produced that meat most likely wouldn't have ever been alive if the dinner table wasn't their final destination." He pointed to the remnants of her meal. "Believe me, you wouldn't want to be around me if all I ever ate were vegan meals like you."

"If you'd just give it an honest try, you might like it."

Seth stabbed the last bite of his baked potato. "Hey, I love a good potato, especially if it's complementing a steak at the time."

"You're hopeless, you know that?"

He nodded happily. "Isn't it wonderful?"

Louie himself came to their table, a slim man in his twenties who'd inherited the restaurant from his father a few years before, the last, at least for the moment, of a long line of Louies.

"How're my two favorite people this evening?"

Gillian said, "We've been discussing the pros and cons of eating meat, red or otherwise."

Louie feigned hurt. "Gillian, lower your voice. All of

our cows live a long, happy life, you know that. Betty Osling raises them on her farm, and I swear, they lead a better life than I do, that's the truth."

"We're not discussing how they live. I'm more concerned with how they die."

Seth shook his head. "Careful, Louie, this is an argument you're not going to win. Trust me, I know."

He patted Seth on the shoulder. "At least you're holding your ground." Louie lowered his voice, then said, "I understand you two were at the shelter today when Vera Hobart died."

"Word gets around town fast, doesn't it," Gillian said. "It's only been a few hours."

"It's all my customers have been talking about. Some of them are calling for the soup kitchen to close. They're afraid it's gotten too dangerous in that section of town. I'm asking for a reason. One of my new girlfriends, Emily Taylor, do you know her? She's been volunteering there for a few weeks, and I'm getting a little worried about her."

Gillian had met Emily the week before, a petite young woman with luminous blue eyes and striking blonde hair down to her waist. "There's no danger down there, Louie."

"Then how do you explain what happened to Vera? I understand one of the homeless women stabbed her for her diamond engagement ring."

Seth said, "We're looking into it ourselves. There's a chance Penny didn't kill her."

Louie frowned. "Somebody stuck that knife in her, it surely wasn't suicide." He brushed his hands together, as if knocking the dust from them. "Enough of death and gloom. Can I interest you two in some dessert? We've got an excellent chocolate mousse tonight, and I saved two servings for you."

Gillian started to refuse, then saw Seth's eyes. "Tell you what, bring us one Mousse and a pair of spoons."

"Excellent, I'll be right back."

As Seth captured the last bit of mousse in the bowl, he

said, "That was wonderful."

Gillian had to agree that the dessert was delicious. "Would you like a glass of wine, or are you ready to go?"

Seth looked at her a moment, then said quietly, "Yes, to both," as he signaled for the check.

"That wasn't a question you could answer yes to, and you know it."

There wasn't a hint of playfulness in his voice as he said, "We can have that drink, but let's do it back at my place."

She nodded, wondering what had brought on his sudden seriousness.

As they drove out to his small tree farm, she said, "You're being awfully quiet."

He nodded, but didn't comment. Gillian wanted to ask him what was on his mind, but it was obvious he wasn't in any mood to talk about it. Instead, she tried to enjoy the ride, watching the lights of town fade into the night as they entered the countryside. By the time they got to Seth's house, it was nearly pitch black; his nearest neighbor was half a mile away, and his caretaker/handyman Grady West didn't believe in burning a watt of energy that wasn't absolutely required. Driving in, they passed Grady's trailer, a double wide his kids had given him a few years before. Gillian knew Grady liked to fuss about how expensive it must have been, but it was readily apparent he'd been pleased by their act of generosity. She said, "Grady must have turned in early tonight."

"Don't bet on it. I saw a glowing ember on the front porch. He's out there smoking, watching the night. Sometimes I sit out there with him, but he gets impatient with me because I can't sit still long enough to listen. If I say two words in an hour, he accuses me of being a motor mouth."

"You two are good friends, aren't you?"

"He was here when I bought the farm, and to be honest with you, I couldn't run the place without him. I keep trying to give him a raise, but Grady swears it'll just go to his head if I do. He gets enough from his pension to send his grown kids money every month, and I suspect that's how they bought him that trailer. Don't ever say anything to Grady about it, though, he's got a streak of pride a mile wide."

They pulled up to Seth's house, a small cottage under a thousand square feet, and a sensor turned on the exterior light. The building had originally been designed as a garage, but Seth had modified the plan into a cozy little home. Gillian knew that a house hadn't come with the Christmas tree farm when he'd bought it, and the cottage had been all he could afford. But even after he got on his feet, Seth refused to add on or build something else entirely. In a way she was glad, the solid little structure suited him. She always loved stepping inside, gazing up at the vaulted canopy, white pine rafters and a tongue-and-groove pine ceiling. A comfortable couch nestled near a babbling copper fountain, and a few feet away, a woodstove stood ready. One bedroom and a single bath were all Seth needed, and he'd been stingy in designing the space so he could leave enough room for his disproportionately large kitchen. It was a cook's kitchen, with exposed copper pans and a hidden pantry stocked with enough food to feed a small army. The last defined space of the structure was a sleeping porch, a small screened-in deck that overlooked the woods.

The night air had a chill to it, and Seth built a small fire in the stove, leaving the door open for aesthetics. The crackling warm scents of the apple wood made a nice contrast with the tinny splashing of the fountain. Gillian moved to the couch while Seth made a pair of drinks.

He stared at the fire a few minutes, then said, "Gillian, we need to talk."

Her heart started beating in her ears, and for a moment she had a hard time breathing. There was an ominous ring to the words. She didn't trust herself to speak, she just nodded and sat attentively on the couch.

Seth's eyes were riveted to the fire as he spoke, his voice full of remembered pain. "I want to tell you about Melissa."

She started to reach for him, to offer what ease she could

to his pain, but before her hand touched her, she knew it would be the wrong thing to do. Instead, she nodded softly and listened.

"You know Melissa died, but what you don't know is that it was my fault." The words were spoken with deathly sadness.

"She had a heart condition, Seth. How could that be your fault?"

He held up a hand. "Melissa never wanted me to be a cop, she was happy being a professor's wife. She only agreed to my career change because she knew it was what I wanted. It was a strain on her, I could see that, but I thought she'd get used to it in time. I was wrong." He took a large swallow of his bourbon, then said in a dull voice, "She died the day I was shot, did you know that?"

Gillian shook her head. She'd been tempted to find out exactly what had happened to Melissa, but she'd forced herself to wait for Seth's explanation. All he'd told her over the years was just that Melissa had had a bad heart.

Seth went on. "I was supposed to be home with her the day she died. In fact, I'd already clocked out when the riot started. Some hotheads were protesting a City Council meeting, and my supervisor asked me to help out with crowd control." He stared into the embers. "Melissa was upset, she'd planned a special dinner for just the two of us, but I had to go, I had to be there in the middle of everything. Well, one of the protesters put a bullet in my leg for my trouble. They never found out who shot me, but they discovered the gun in a trash can two blocks away from City Hall. Anyway, a camera crew from Channel Three was reporting live on the protest, and they happened to catch me falling to the pavement with a bullet in me.

"Melissa was watching television, worried about me as usual." He choked back a tear, and Gillian finally did touch him on the shoulder.

"You don't have to tell me anything more, Seth."

"Just let me finish, okay," he choked out. "I didn't find

out she was dead until I was in the surgery recovery room. They didn't even want to tell me then, but I couldn't figure out why they wouldn't let her in to see me, so finally the chief told me. He'd gone to the house personally to tell Melissa I was going to be all right, and he was worried when she didn't come to the door. He looked in through the kitchen window and saw her lying on the floor. By the time he got to her, it was too late."

"Seth, I'm so sorry." The words were inadequate, but they were the best she could do. Gillian had known Seth bore guilt over his wife's death, but she'd had no idea just how much. It explained a lot of things about him that she hadn't understood.

He finished the bourbon with a single gulp, then said, "That's not the worst of it. I made them bring the doctor who'd examined her to see me in my room. I had to know for sure if the strain of seeing me shot on live television had killed her. He told me matter-of-factly that it was bound to happen sooner or later, not to beat myself up about it. Then he added almost as an afterthought that the childbirth would have endangered her life more than my shooting had. I thought he was mistaken, then accused him of lying, Melissa would have told me if she'd been pregnant. He shook his head sadly and told me she was just six weeks pregnant. That explained the special dinner she'd prepared; she was going to tell me the night she died. We'd discussed having kids, but the doctors all told her it would be too dangerous. Melissa didn't care, she wanted a family more than anything else." Seth's eyes were filled with tears, as were Gillian's. The crackling flames were surreal through her misty vision, but she couldn't stand looking at Seth, seeing the pain on his face. In a voice barely audible, he said, "She didn't even get to tell me she was pregnant. I stole that from her."

Gillian wrapped her arms around him, pulling him into her embrace. His sobs wracked his body, and she joined him, mourning his loss with him. Finally, drained of all emotion, they stayed entwined, Gillian softly stroking his hair, murmuring gentle words in his ear. When he finally pulled away, he rubbed the last tears from his eyes, then stood and laid a few more small logs in the fire. He turned and looked at her intently. "So now you know why I'm like I am. Still want to be with me?"

Gillian said earnestly, "For as long as you'll have me."

He nodded, and a smile of relief crossed his face.

At that moment, the window behind Seth shattered in an explosion that filled the air with deadly slivers and shards of glass.

Chapter 7

Seth dove to the hardwood floor, pulling Gillian along with him in one complete motion. As he was falling on top of her to the floor, he heard another shot whiz through the air, burying itself into the wall behind where he'd been standing a moment before.

He whispered, "Are you okay?"

"I guess so. What happened?"

"Somebody's shooting at us. Wait here. I'm going to get my revolver."

As he started to get up, Gillian held tightly to his shirt. "I'm not armed, either, and I'm not about to hang around and wait for whoever's out there to come in. I'm going with you. You can have your revolver; I want the shotgun."

Seth had forgotten in the heat of the moment that Gillian was at least as good with weapons as he was himself. Her father had taught her well, from guns to personal self-defense to a host of tricks and techniques he was still discovering.

He nodded. "Okay, keep yourself low and watch out for broken glass." Seth led her back to his bedroom, and after retrieving his .38 revolver from the night table, he reached under his bed and pulled out his twelve-gauge shotgun. Both weapons were loaded and ready to fire; there were no children ever in his home, and Seth didn't believe a gun was worth much unless it was ready to fire when he needed it. It still made him feel better when Gillian opened the breach and checked to be sure it was loaded. He did the same with his revolver, spinning the cylinder, then slapping it back in place. Keeping his voice low, he said, "I'm going to turn the lights off in the living room so we're not such an obvious target. I'll be back in a second."

She nodded as he slowly crept back into the room, his eyes scanning constantly for any sign of the shooter. As he spied the damage, he felt angry that someone had tried to hurt

Gillian and him in his home, his sanctuary. They'd pay a little extra for that, he'd see to that personally no matter what else happened. He flicked the light switch down, and the cottage was darkened, though the glow from the wood stove still gave off more illumination than he liked. Seth looked at the door, then back at the flames. That escape path wouldn't do at all.

Gillian was waiting for him in the darkness of his room. He could see the barrel of the shotgun lower as she recognized him.

"What's our next move?" she asked. Her words were spoken in the same tone she might have used asking where he wanted to eat that night, and Seth found himself admiring her calm courage.

In response, he slid the bedroom window open. "If we go out the front door, I've got a sneaking suspicion we're going to get an unhealthy welcome." He patted his leg, which throbbed gently under the strain of falling. "I've been shot before, and I don't recommend it."

Gillian said, "You're not going to do your leg any good by climbing out windows, either. Let me go out and look around."

He grinned in spite of the tension of the situation. "What, and let you have all of the fun? We're in this together, remember? I don't think so. I've been walking a lot lately, this should be a piece of cake." Still, he pulled the chair from his small desk and placed it directly under the window. While it was true he'd been exercising his bad leg more and more every day, it wasn't in nearly as good a shape as he was trying to lead Gillian to believe. He'd be stiff and sore in the morning, there was no doubt about that, but if he didn't do something about the situation outside immediately, he wouldn't have to worry about that, or anything else.

He got out of the window with more grace than he'd expected. Gillian seemed to glide out behind him, and he slid the window softly back in place. A waxing moon was out, giving enough light to show the way, but not the brutal illuminating glare of a full moon. They gave themselves a few minutes to let their eyes grow accustomed to the dark when Seth heard a branch snap ten yards away from them. Almost instantly, he heard a voice call out gently, "It's Grady. I'd appreciate it if you'd both point those barrels in other places besides the space I'm currently occupying."

Grady came closer, and Seth said, "Have you seen anything out here?"

"Not a soul. Whoever took those shots at you was in a supreme hurry to haul tail out of here. My guess is they're long gone."

Gillian laughed softly. "But you're not sure, or you wouldn't be slinking around the woods in the middle of the night with a rifle in your hands."

Grady said, "I haven't gotten to this age by taking too many things for granted."

Gillian said, "We'd better call the police, hadn't we? Shouldn't they know somebody took two shots at us?"

Seth shook his head. "I can hear the sheriff now. He'll most likely just blame it on kids out sowing some wild oats. Besides, I'm not willing to wait around for him to send a patrol car out here. If the shooter is still on the farm, I want to find him myself. A shrieking siren's going to send him running for the hills. The three of us can handle this ourselves."

Grady's head bobbed with his ascent.

In thirty minutes, they'd patrolled most of the land surrounding the house, and everyone reluctantly agreed that Grady had been right; the shooter was long gone.

Gillian said, "Do you agree with Seth, Grady? Is calling the police a waste of time?"

Grady seemed to study the matter a few moments before speaking. Gillian knew him to be a thoughtful man who never appeared to do anything without considering the possibilities first. "I believe I do. At the moment, we can't be sure the vandal theory isn't the correct one, high school boys have been known to get drunk a time or two, and every last one of them seem to be armed these days. I'm just not sure what good it would do to tell anyone about this."

"It might keep whoever was here from coming back. That's got to be worth something."

Grady shrugged. "I doubt it, not when he's bound to know we're armed and waiting for him. I don't know about you, but I don't relish the prospect of a policeman on duty here all the time, even if they did believe us. You're forgetting something, not every cop in the world is as good as your father was. No, I'd have to agree with Seth. Let's play this one by ear and see what happens." He turned to Seth. "I'll take care of that window in the morning, I've been itching for something to do around here. It might get a little chilly tonight, what with that open window and all. I'll get some cardboard up to block most of the breeze, that should help some."

Seth was about to say something when Gillian cut him off. "Don't worry about it, Grady, we'll just sleep at my place tonight." She turned to Seth and said, "If that's all right with you, that is."

Seth smiled. "I guess I could live with it, though I must admit I've had more sincere invitations in my life." He patted Grady on the shoulder. "You know where to reach me if you need me for anything, anything at all. You going to be okay out here by yourself?"

"Seth, I was taking care of myself before you were nothing but a gleam in your daddy's eye, don't you worry about me."

Seth took the shotgun from Gillian's hands and gave it to Grady. "Look out for this for me, will you? I don't like leaving it in the house without being there."

Grady nodded as he swung the rifle to his shoulder, but not before checking the breach himself. "I'll keep her by my bedside, she'll be safe enough."

Seth tucked his own revolver into his jacket. He decided he'd keep it handy while they were snooping around. Truthfully, he always felt a little naked walking around without it. Not that he'd ever drawn his weapon as a cop, it just felt better being on him, just in case.

As they drove to Gillian's loft, she said, "Are you sure Grady's going to be okay? He's not getting any younger, you know."

He touched Gillian's hand. "He can take care of himself."

"Seth, who would want to take two shots at you?"

"Well, unless you've got an ardent suitor stashed away somewhere who's jealous of the competition, I can't think of anybody I've made mad enough to take a shot at me. How about you? As I recall, you were standing right beside me when that window shattered."

"I'm serious, Seth. Do you think we asked too many questions today? Is someone trying to scare us off from snooping around?"

"If they are, they're going about it the wrong way entirely. The best way to get a cop's suspicions going is to try to scare him off a case."

She said gently, "You're not a cop any more, remember?"

"Try telling my instincts that. Truthfully, I don't think there's a chance in the world that was random tonight, but I can't for the life of me figure out what we did that merited the target practice."

"At least our suspect list is narrowed down to Bradley and Jason."

Seth shook his head. "I wouldn't bet on it. We asked Lex a ton of questions, too, and from what I've heard about her, it's probably all over town by now that we're not buying Penny as the murderer. This could have been nothing more than a preemptive strike to stop us from confronting the real murderer."

"Somehow I'm guessing it didn't work, did it?"

Seth laughed gently. "It failed miserably. I'm more determined than ever to get to the truth behind Vera's death. I'm not about to let a couple of stray bullets get in my way."

He glanced over at Gillian. "If it's getting a little rougher than you expected, there's no shame in backing out of this. I certainly won't think less of you for it."

Gillian said sternly, "And what do you think Frank Hurley would think of his baby girl if she backed down from an invitation to a fight with a bad guy? I appreciate your concern, but I want to see this through just as much as you do."

Seth pulled her as close to him as their seat-belts would allow. "You're quite a woman, Gillian."

"Thanks for noticing," she said as he pulled up in front of her loft.

Before they got out of the truck, Gillian said, "Seth, somebody's in the bushes by the door."

"Are you sure? It could have been the wind moving the branches."

Her voice was firm. "I'm positive. To the left of the doorway, five feet into the shadows. You can't see it now, but somebody's there, take my word for it. Let's go see what they want."

There was no doubt in Gillian's voice as she spoke. Seth pulled the revolver from his jacket, then took off his coat even though the temperature was dropping steadily outside. He arranged the jacket over his hand holding the gun, fussing with it for a few seconds before he was satisfied with the arrangement. "Let's go. I want you to stay behind me, just in case." He waited until Gillian got out on his side of the truck, then Seth started toward the door, his gun pointed directly toward the shape Gillian had seen.

Seth tightened his grip on the handle of his revolver, and he could feel that heightened sense of awareness that came with his adrenaline rushes. It was a slice of the best and the worst parts of being a cop, knowing that danger was just a breath away. Twenty paces from the door, he could make out the bulky shadow that shouldn't have been there. Calling out firmly, he said, "Come out of the shadows. I've got a gun trained on your gut, and if you don't do exactly what I say, I promise you, you're going to die."

"Wait, don't shoot, it's just me." A man in old clothes came out of the shadows, and Seth saw that it was Ace, their homeless friend.

As he put his jacket back on and tucked the gun safely away, Seth said, "That's a bad habit you've got, hiding in the bushes like that. With the night we've had, you're lucky I didn't shoot you on general principles."

"I couldn't just sit on the doorstep, could I? I'd be in jail for loitering, most likely. A police car's been by twice since I got here."

Gillian asked, "Did they get out and come to the door?"

"No, they just cruised by, but both times the cop's eyes went straight to your place." He paused a moment, then said, "What kind of night have you had that you're ready to shoot at shadows?"

"Somebody took a few shots at my house," Seth said. "I don't appreciate their attempts to redecorate. What brings you out here? Have you learned anything new?"

Ace grinned with his perfect teeth. "I found Penny."

In ten minutes, the three of them were standing in an alley behind one of Jackson's Ferry's economy grocery stores. Seth touched Gillian's shoulder with his free hand; in the other, he held his revolver, undisguised and uncovered. The streets and alleyways of downtown at night were no place to wander around unarmed. There were too many nooks a mugger could use for ambush, too many crannies to drag the victim into. The police only made a perfunctory effort to patrol the area at night. There was just too much space to handle, and too few men and women to watch over it effectively.

Seth said softly, "Are you sure she'd down this alley?"

"She was when I left her." Ace studied the gap in the buildings between the grocery store and an abandoned warehouse next door, then found the passage he was looking for. "Through here."

As Ace ducked between a stack of flat wooden pallets and the cinderblock wall, Seth motioned for Gillian to go ahead of him. As he made his way through the makeshift tunnel, he kept glancing backward. If this was a trap, it would be the perfect place to come at him. There was barely room to turn around, let alone aim his revolver accurately.

The pallet maze finally ended and opened up onto a small alcove. Seth was surprised to see a light inside the cave-like space. The maze must have blocked every stray ray of light from the street. As he stepped inside, Ace moved a flattened cardboard refrigerator box over the opening where they'd just entered. It made for a snug harbor from the night. He saw that the light was coming from an open Sterno can, its flames dancing and flickering on the surface. It was warm, too, and Seth wondered about proper ventilation. It would be a fine dance sleeping there between hypothermia and suffocation.

Penny was sitting in front of the flame, her eyes on him. "Have you come to arrest me? Ace told me you wanted to help me."

Seth realized he still had his revolver in his hand. As he tucked it back into his jacket pocket, he said, "I'm not a cop, any more, Penny, you know that. We're here to help."

She shook her head. "Nobody can help me now. The cops already made up their minds that I killed her."

As Seth and Gillian sat across from the Sterno can fire, Gillian said, "That's why we've been looking into what happened. It's hard, though, without knowing your side of the story. What happened today?"

Penny said, "I was getting ready to find Ace so we could get in line at the Soup Kitchen like we always do when this woman came up to me and started talking."

"Was it Vera Hobart?"

Penny shrugged. "I couldn't tell you. I think she volunteered a time or two, I believe I recognized her voice. Anyway, she was wearing a big floppy hat, and she had a pair of black sunglasses on, too. She was dressed nice, too, but that's all I could say." Apologetically, she added, "I'm horrible with names, and not much better with faces. My memory's just about shot when it comes to stuff like that." She looked at her hands as she said, "Too much to drink for too many years, I guess." After a moment's silent reflection, she continued. "Anyway, this woman presses something in my hand and says, 'I don't need this anymore. Maybe it'll bring you better luck than it brought me.' I looked down in my hand and found this." Penny held up something that glittered in the fire's dancing light.

It had to be Vera Hobart's engagement ring.

Gillian said, "So she just gave it to you out of the blue?"

Penny turned to Ace. "See? I told you nobody'd believe me. I can't hardly believe it myself, it sounds so crazy. Nobody'd just give their ring away like that."

Seth said softly, "We believe you, Penny. We're here, aren't we? Now Ace told us someone stole your knife a few days ago. Can you tell us anything else about that?"

Penny started to wring her hands together. "Ace shouldn't have said that. He--."

Ace's voice was stern as he said, "Penny, I'm not going to let them hang you for this."

Her voice softened as she touched his shoulder. "Lying's not going to get us out of it, I know that much, though I thank you for the effort." Penny turned back to Seth, her gaze steady. "I didn't even know it was gone until I heard that woman had been stabbed, and that's the honest truth."

"When was the last time you know you had it? Think hard, it's important."

"Don't you think I've been trying? I don't know. I just don't know." Her last words were said in a whimper. She burrowed into Ace's chest and started to cry. As Ace stroked her knotted hair, he cooed softly to her, "It's going to be all right, Penny, it's going to be all right."

Seth had a feeling they weren't going to get anything else out of Penny for a while, she was too distraught. He couldn't afford to wait around until she was ready to talk, either. He and Gillian could be arrested as accessories after the fact if there was the slightest suspicion they were keeping Penny's location from the police. She was the prime suspect in a murder investigation, and he knew that regardless of his relationship with Kline, the sheriff would have no choice but to go after them. Seth made up his mind that there was only one thing they could do, but he was certain nobody in the alcove would like what he had to say. Taking a deep breath, he said, "Penny, you're going to have to turn yourself in to the police tonight."

Before anyone else could say a word, Penny's crying jag became a mournful wail, and Seth was certain no thicknesses of cardboard would be able to contain the noise. As Ace tried to calm her, he said, "I thought you were going to try to keep her out of jail, not lead her to a cell."

"Ace, think about it. Penny's in danger out here. Whoever killed Vera is going to want her dead. She's the only one who can testify that she's innocent. Penny's going to be a lot safer in jail than she will be here on the street."

Penny stopped crying and said in a ragged voice, "I'm afraid. I don't want to be locked up again."

Gillian tried to calm her. "It's okay, Penny, don't worry. You can come stay with me until this mess is all over."

Seth snapped, "Gillian, that's not an option. I'm not going to have you arrested as an accessory."

"She didn't kill Vera, Seth."

Now what was he going to do? He recognized the resolute tone of Gillian's voice, and knew she wouldn't be easily dissuaded from her stand. Sometimes Gillian's Mother-To-The-World syndrome was a real pain in the rear. "How much good are you going to be able to do Penny if you're in jail? How many meals at the Soup Kitchen can you serve from your cell? You want to help the world, you're not going to do it from behind bars."

"I can't let her just go to jail. I won't."

Penny reached across the low flame and patted Gillian's hand. "Your heart's in the right place, but he's right. How do you think I'd feel if you went to jail because of me? I won't let you do that."

Ace said, "I'll stay with her here, she'll be safe enough."

Seth sighed. "So you're not willing to turn yourself over to the police?"

"You call the cops, and they'll come here and shoot me. I'll never make it to the jail."

Seth asked, "Is that what you're afraid of? What if I could guarantee that you make it to the jail safely? Would you go then?"

Penny looked at Ace. "My mind's all cloudy. What should I do, Ace?"

He seemed to think about it for hours, though Seth knew that only a few minutes had passed when he said, "As much as I hate to admit it, Penny, Seth's right. You're not safe out here. I'm sorry, I can't protect you." Ace turned to Seth. "How can you be so sure nothing will happen to her before she gets to the jail?"

"We've got a friend who's an attorney; she handles things like this all the time. Let me call her, she can be here in twenty minutes."

Penny shook her head. "We have to do it in the morning. I can't handle this tonight, I'm sorry, I just can't." Then she buried her head back into Ace's chest and started to cry again, this time more softly than before.

Ace looked at him with pleading in his eyes. "What do you say, Seth, is tomorrow morning soon enough? She's not in any shape to go anywhere tonight, let alone jail."

"I don't like it, Ace; there are too many variables on the street. She'll be safer in protective custody."

Ace frowned. "You might think of it as protective custody, but you can bet the police are going to be thinking of it as arresting a murderer. She's fragile, more fragile than you could know. I'm not sure she could take it, in the state she's in right now."

Gillian said, "Seth, she's lived on the streets for years. Is one more night really going to hurt anything?"

Reluctantly, Seth agreed. "First thing tomorrow morning

we'll be back with an attorney. Don't leave here, for any reason. Do you understand me?"

Ace nodded. "Can you find your way out?"

Gillian said softly, "We'll be fine. Just look out for her."

"I promise. See you in the morning." He studied Seth a moment, then asked, "This lawyer, is he any good?"

"She's the best I know."

Ace continued. "I could get my hands on some money, if you know anybody else."

Seth wondered how much Ace had at his disposal. It couldn't be much, given the conditions in which he lived. Still, the gesture was sincere.

"I'd trust her with my life."

"That's good enough for me."

As Seth and Gillian drove back to her loft, Gillian said, "That was brilliant, thinking of Allison. Do you think she's home now?"

"She's married to her work. If I know Allison, she's probably still at her office."

"Why don't we swing by and see her?"

Seth stifled a yawn. "To be honest with you, I'm too tired to keep my eyes open."

"Ten minutes, that's all it'll take."

Seth grinned at her. "You're a slave driver, you know that, don't you?"

She smiled. "I'm just trying to keep you motivated." Her face clouded a moment as she said, "I'm not afraid of going to jail for Penny, you know that, don't you?"

"It's not a matter of being afraid," Seth said wearily. "I need you free so you can help me investigate."

Gillian raised an eyebrow. "So you admit I'm handy to have around?"

"There's never been any doubt in my mind." He winked at her, then said, "Of course, if they allowed conjugal visits, I might be willing to bend on my position on jail time."

Gillian laughed as they pulled up in front of Allison Cole's law firm. She gave him a kiss that warmed him to his toes and wiped the growing cobwebs from his mind. "What was that for?"

"I just wanted to be sure I had your full attention before we saw Allison."

"If that's your reaction to her, we should see the lady lawyer more often."

Chapter 8

Gillian knew bringing Allison Cole in on the situation was the wisest thing to do, but she'd hesitated saying anything until Seth had brought it up himself. It wasn't that there was any rivalry between the two women for Seth's attention; Gillian was self-assured enough to know that he was happy being with her. Still, there was no doubt in her mind that if for some reason she wasn't in Seth's life any more, Allison would be more than happy to step in and fill the void. If nothing else, it gave the two women something in common; each admired the other's taste in men.

They found Allison working at her desk, her long auburn hair pulled back in an unlawyerly bright orange scrunchie. Though she wore a gray double-breasted suit with a short skirt, Gillian could see the pristine tennis shoes on her feet tucked under her desk. Allison was concentrating on a contract on her desktop, her delicate nose wrinkled in obvious irritation, and didn't notice as they came in.

Gillian said, "Did we come at a bad time?"

Allison moved a strand of hair from her eyes as she saw them, and intensified her smile when she realized Seth was there. "No, come in. To be honest, I could use the break." She tapped the legal document in front of her. "One of my clients asked me to go over this contract his son signed. This thing must have been drawn up by a first year law student, it's got more loopholes in it than the old tax code."

Seth said, "Allison, we need your help."

She stood up, gently smoothing the lines of her skirt. Whether she intended it or not, Gillian saw Seth's eyes go to Allison's long slender legs for a moment, the lawyer's most outstanding feature. Gillian smiled despite herself; Allison was a master of body language, a skill that had to help her immeasurably in her job as a trial lawyer. That's how Gillian and Seth had met her. Upon graduating from Duke Law

School, Richard Nixon's alma mater no less, she'd moved to Jackson's Ferry and set up a small practice despite the rumored offers of partnerships throughout the big cities of the South. Allison had told them on more than one occasion that she was a small town girl at heart, and the large metropolitan areas made her nervous. Gillian doubted anything in the world could make Allison Cole nervous, but nevertheless, she'd been a boon to the community. Allison was the type of attorney it was getting rarer to see graduating from major law schools these days; she was more interested in the causes she could champion than the fees she could charge.

"Whatever I can do, I'm here for you." Allison caught Gillian's eye and added, "Both of you."

"That's why we're here," Gillian nodded. "Have you heard about the Vera Hobart murder?"

"Are you kidding? Word spread through the courthouse faster than CNN could have reported it. It's on all the Charlotte television stations. They're saying a homeless woman killed her. Somebody you know?"

"Her name's Penny. We know her from the soup kitchen, and neither one of us think there's a chance in the world she actually did it."

That caught Allison's attention. She leaned against the edge of her desk, showing off her marvelous legs to their best advantage. As Gillian studied her, she realized the movement was most likely an unconscious one developed over the course of her life. "From what I've heard in the rumor mill, the police can't find her. That doesn't project the proper air of innocence, if you know what I mean."

"We know where she is," Seth said softly. "She's willing to turn herself in, but she's afraid of the police."

Allison said, "This isn't the Old South any more, the cops don't beat confessions out of their prime suspects." She grinned. "At least not with me around. Where is she? Can I speak with her?"

Gillian said, "We couldn't get her to come with us. I

don't know how reliable a witness she's going to appear to be, she's shaky on a lot of things."

"Don't worry about that, by the time I'm through with her, she'll look like June Cleaver. Do you at least have a last name on her so I can run some preliminary searches on her?"

Gillian shook her head. "Sorry, most of our clientele at the soup kitchen go by nicknames or first names only. You'll have to ask her tomorrow morning, if you're willing to help her, that is."

"There was never any doubt." She tapped a pencil in her hand. "I'm not sure waiting is the best strategy. Why don't we take care of this tonight?"

"She couldn't handle it," Gillian said, keeping her eyes averted from Seth. "How do things look for you in the morning?"

"Let me check my appointment book and I'll see what I've got scheduled for tomorrow."

As she slid past them and walked into her secretary's office, Allison said from the doorway, "You two run into the most interesting people." She scanned her open schedule and said, "I don't have anything here until ten tomorrow morning. Can you get Penny here by eight?"

"We'll do our best. I'm afraid she won't even have the customary dollar to retain your services."

Allison laughed. "It won't be the first time I had to loan my fee to a client."

Seth smiled and said, "We really appreciate this. We'll let you get back to work. Sorry to have disturbed you."

"I was glad for the break. See you in the morning."

As they left and headed back to Gillian's loft, she said, "You didn't tell her about the shooting tonight. Don't you think she has a right to know it might be dangerous taking this case?"

"It's possible those shots were nothing more than a prank. The kids around here have been getting a little wild lately. I've seen them do worse things than this."

"Don't talk yourself into anything, Seth, you weren't so

sure when we were on the floor. We've got to tell Allison in the morning. She has a right to know."

He rubbed Gillian's shoulder gently with his free hand as he drove. "You're right, I'm sorry. It's one thing for us to take chances, we know what's going on. I should have told Allison. We'll fix that first thing in the morning."

As they drove up to the loft's main door, Seth asked gently, "See anybody else lurking in the bushes?"

"No, but I've got to admit, I'll feel better when we're locked safely in upstairs."

He smiled at her warmly. "Personally, I won't feel better until we're both under the covers."

"I've got a feeling that doesn't have anything to do with feeling safe."

"Guilty as charged."

The next morning, Gillian reached for Seth but found that he was already up. She loved it when he stayed the night, something Seth rarely did. Though they often shared each other's beds, they were both quite sensitive about intruding on each other's personal space. It was an arrangement that under normal circumstances they were both happy to continue, but Gillian had to admit, having Seth around in times of trouble was an added comfort to her. It wasn't so much because he was a man, or even a cop for that matter; he was company, and good company at that. Gillian was normally quite happy in her own skin, spending time in silence and solitude, but at the moment, his presence made her feel a little bit less alone in the world.

He was making omelets when she walked into the kitchen, stopping first to throw on an oversized T-shirt Seth kept at her place.

He whistled as she modeled it for him, then said, "My Fruit of the Loom's never looked so good."

She curtsied. "Thank you, sir. Are those your famous omelets I smell?"

"I knew you'd wake up the second they hit the pan."

"It's the best alarm clock in the world."

As he slid a plate in front of her, Seth said, "Hope I didn't keep you awake last night. I had a hard time sleeping."

"Nightmares again?" Gillian knew that Seth still suffered from bad dreams about Melissa, and now that she knew about Melissa's pregnancy, it started to make even more sense to her. Seth was still mourning the loss of his child as well as his first wife. She wished she could ease some of his pain, but there was nothing she could do but be there for him.

He obviously read the tone in her voice and the sympathy in her eyes. "No, not about that. I'm worried about Penny. I can't help thinking it was a mistake leaving her out on the streets alone."

Gillian said, "She wasn't alone, Ace was with her, remember? Seth, you saw her eyes. If we'd insisted she come with us, I think she would have snapped. Sleeping in her own environment was probably the best thing she could do to calm her nerves."

"Yeah, I guess you're right." He pointed to her omelet. "You'd better eat that before it gets cold." As she took her first bite, Seth said, "You know, that egg had a mother, too."

Gillian took a sip of hot tea, then said, "Not that it knew. I eat fish, too, but there was no maternal bond there, either. I won't touch veal, beef or chicken."

"You don't know what you're missing." He took a bite, then added, "Not bad, but it could really use some sausage."

She said, "Are you telling me you're surprised you didn't find some in my refrigerator?"

"I can always hope."

After breakfast, Seth changed into some clothes he kept at her loft while Gillian cleaned up the breakfast dishes. That was part of their deal; Seth cooked and Gillian cleaned up afterward.

They were just getting ready to walk out the door when the doorbell rang.

Gillian was surprised to find Allison Cole on her doorstep. "Come on in, Allison. I thought we were going to meet at your office."

"There's been a change of plans. Is Seth here?"

He came around the corner, buttoning the last button of his sweater. "Right here. What's up?"

"I stopped by the police station on my way into the office this morning, and it looks like we've got trouble."

"More than we do already? How bad could it be?"

Allison frowned. "The police have a witness who's willing to swear under oath he saw a woman plunge the knife in Vera's chest just outside the soup kitchen."

Seth said, "Come on, Allison. You know as well as I do that eyewitnesses are usually the most unreliable form of evidence there is. Besides, somebody hanging around in that section of town can't be the most reliable witness in the world. He could have been mistaken."

Allison said, "That's the problem. It turns out he's a seminary student from the Episcopal teaching satellite in town. He was spending three days on the streets to get a feel for the people he wants to minister to. It's going to be tough discrediting a priest helping the homeless."

Gillian said, "But even so, he hasn't identified Penny, has he?"

"No, but that's why they've been so eager to find her. They've been wanting to do a line up since the murder, but they can't do that without Penny. It seems the priest came forward just after you left the soup kitchen yesterday, and the police have been holding him on ice without saying a word to anyone that he even existed. Folks, our plans have changed. We've got to go get Penny now and take her to police headquarters now."

They decided to take Allison's car, a second-hand Volvo, since everybody wouldn't fit in Seth's truck or Gillian's car when they picked up Ace and Penny. When they got to the place they'd left them the night before, Seth said to Allison, "You wait here. Gillian and I will go get her and tell her the situation. She might not react too well to you without a little warning. Penny hates surprises."

Allison nodded, and it appeared to Gillian that she'd rather stay safely locked up in her car anyway. It was something that had taken Gillian time to get used to herself. The environs were not what she'd been used to for much of her life, and she was still a little uncertain every time she visited the downtown area. Seth had assured her that he felt an itch between his shoulder blades himself whenever they walked the streets, but she figured he was just trying to make her feel better. She couldn't imagine him being afraid of anything, especially not an overt threat. He was the kind of person who handled situations face-to-face, with no nonsense.

They walked through the maze of pallets, this time having an easier time in the early light of dawn.

When they got to the comfortable cardboard grotto, they found it deserted.

Ace and Penny were gone.

There was no sign of a struggle, not that they could tell in the jumble of bedding and discarded items inside the den.

Gillian said, "Seth, you told Ace not to leave until we got here."

"Let's not jump to conclusions, Gillian. There could be a hundred reasons why they're gone." He looked around the space, then said, "I'd look for a clue as to where they went, but I can't even tell if they were forced out or they left willingly." He kicked at some debris. "It doesn't look like a crime scene, at least not at first glance."

"We can't be sure, though, can we?"

He squeezed her shoulder. "Gillian, there's not much in this world we can be certain about it, is there?"

She touched his hand lightly. She was sure of how much she loved him, but it wasn't the time or the place to tell him that.

Seth said, "Don't worry, I'm sure they'll turn up."

After wending their way out of the maze, they saw Allison staring at the entrance. Gillian heard the automatic door locks click open the second before her hand touched the doorknob.

Once they were inside the car, Allison asked, "So, are they coming or not? We can't wait too much longer."

Seth took a deep breath, then said, "They're gone. Any chance the police found them last night?"

"No, they would have told me this morning. I stretched the truth a little, based on our conversation, and told them Penny had already hired me as her attorney. She did, in fact, through you, but I didn't want to admit I'd never met her to the sheriff. He was obligated to tell me if he was holding her, but he repeated emphatically that she wasn't even being charged with the crime yet, they were just looking for her for questioning and a line-up. I hinted that I'd be producing her shortly. This is going to make me look bad."

Seth said evenly, "There's more than your reputation at stake here. I don't like the fact that they're gone."

Allison said, "I'm concerned, too. Do you have any idea where she might be?"

"Not yet, but we'll find her. There's nothing you can do here at the moment. Why don't you go on in to your office, and we'll call you the second we find her."

Allison looked incredulous. "You want me to just leave you here, without a car or anything?"

Gillian knew Seth had his revolver with him, not that he expected to need it downtown. He said, "Allison, we know these people, we've been around them for years. They trust us, but they don't know you. You have to believe us, we'll be fine."

Allison shrugged. "If you're sure." After they were out of the car, she rolled down her window and said, "Would you at least take my cellular phone in case you need me?"

Seth held up his hands. "Gillian's got hers with her all the time. Don't worry, we'll be fine. No matter what, we'll check in with you before noon."

"Okay, if you're sure."

As she drove away, Seth said, "Did she seem a little

jumpy to you this morning?"

Gillian smiled. "She's not exactly used to being downtown in this particular section of Jackson's Ferry. It takes a while getting used to it."

Seth wrapped an arm around her waist. "It didn't take you any time at all."

She pulled closer. "Haven't you heard? I'm special."

"Gillian, there's never been any doubt of that."

"Any ideas where we should start looking?"

"No, I just figured we'd walk around a little and see what we could come up with. To be honest, I don't have the slightest idea where they've gone. We'd better find them, though. The sheriff's not going to be too happy with either one of us when he finds out we let her get away."

"I'm sorry, Seth, you were right. We should have forced her to turn herself in last night."

He only shrugged in reply.

After two hours of walking through the streets, questioning an acquaintance or two along the way, Seth and Gillian were no closer to finding Ace and Penny than they had when they'd started looking.

Finally Seth said, "I give up. It's as if they've disappeared." He glanced at his watch. "The soup kitchen's due to open soon, and we're scheduled to work again. I'm hoping Penny and Ace will show up there. To be honest with you, I don't know what else to do."

They worked their shift at the soup kitchen, always keeping one eye on the door hoping that Ace or Penny would show up.

They never did.

As Gillian finished wiping down the serving counter, she said, "I've got a bad feeling about this, Seth. I've never known Ace to miss a meal in all the times I've volunteered here."

"I admit it, I'm starting to get worried myself. They should have turned up by now. Maybe Penny started getting cold feet, or Ace could have been worried they were too easy to find and decided to move her. Either way, I don't think we'll find them until they're ready to come forward themselves."

"So what do we do in the meantime?"

"There's not much else we can do. Until they show up, we need to pick up the threads of what we were doing yesterday and see if there was anyone in Vera's life who wanted to see her dead."

Chapter 9

Seth didn't want to admit it to Gillian, but there was something else weighing on his mind. With all that had gone on in the past twenty-four hours, he was beginning to wonder if he should have left Grady out at the farm by himself. The man was getting older, though he'd deny the accusation no matter what the evidence was to the contrary. Over the past few years, the two of them had become much more than employer and worker. There was a special bond there, a common outlook on the insanity of the world around them. Seth had found a spiritual brother in Grady, someone who shared his old fashioned values of hard work, respect for God and Country, and a firm sense of self-reliance.

Seth said, "Before we talk to anyone else, I want to stop off at the farm and see how Grady's doing."

"I thought you said he could take care of himself."

"I just want to see if he's found anything since daylight. He's the best hunter I know. If there's a clue in the woods, Grady's found it by now."

As they drove out to Seth's farm, Gillian said, "I still can't believe such a sweet old man is a cold-blooded murderer. How anyone can kill Bambi's father is beyond me."

"Gillian, he doesn't do it for the sport, Grady lives most of the year off what he shoots in deer season. He's an excellent shot, and there's no suffering involved. If he didn't thin the population, we'd be overrun by deer. Believe me, they'd destroy my farm in a single season if Grady didn't hunt them and help keep their population in check. A buck's favorite snack is one of my Christmas trees."

"But you don't hunt yourself."

"Just because I don't doesn't mean I can't understand why someone else does. I admit it, I'd have a hard time pulling the trigger, but if it meant eating or starving, I believe

I could do it. The only hunter I'm against is the one who's an amateur at it. Either they can't shoot straight and the poor creature suffers before someone can put it out of its misery or they kill the deer and leave the carcass after they claim the antlered rack as their trophy. Grady's threatened to put a bullet in a hunter or two himself because of that, and I've seen him disarm men twice his size and destroy their expensive weapons right in front of them."

"I don't care what you say, Seth, I still think it's barbaric."

He shrugged, knowing that this was just one more of the subjects they'd long ago agreed to disagree about. They'd both realized early on into their relationship that there were many points of contention between them. The only way they could stay together was to discuss everything in the open, but neither could afford to take offense at the other's point of view. The pact was tenuous at times, but all in all it had managed to keep their relationship strong.

Grady was inside Seth's house patching a spot of drywall when they got to the farm. The handyman nodded his greeting and pointed to a section of pine on the table. "I had to cut out part of a stud to get one bullet out without destroying the markings." He held up a hand. "Don't worry, I patched it, good as new. This time next week you won't be able to find the spot where the bullet went in."

"What about the other shot?"

Grady flipped a piece of lead into his hands. "It's pretty well ruined. It nicked your stove pipe and flattened out when it hit the wall."

Seth picked up the piece of pine that held the other bullet and said, "Looks like a 30.06 slug to me."

Grady nodded. "About half the boys around here use it for deer hunting. I noticed something interesting, though." He didn't say another word, just watched Seth carefully. There was a gleam in the older man's eye, and Seth knew he was being challenged. He studied the position of the drywall patches, the nicked surface of the wood stove's pipe, then stared outside. He noticed Gillian watching with fascination, but she didn't interrupt.

After a few moments, Seth said, "Whoever shot at us wasn't trying to kill us. It was just a warning, or else a badly placed shot."

As Grady nodded his approval, Gillian said, "What makes you say that? Those shots seemed pretty real to me."

Seth explained. "The first bullet, the one that took out the window, was high. Look at where it grazed the pipe. From where I was standing, it would have been a real fluke for it to have hit me."

Gillian pointed to the patch Grady had been working on. "What about this one? It would have blown your head off."

"I seem to recall a delay in the two shots."

Gillian nodded her understanding. "So the shooter waited until we hit the floor before putting another one into the house. I'm impressed, gentlemen."

Grady shook his head. "Don't be impressed with me. It took me the better part of an hour to figure out what he realized in less than a minute."

Seth patted Grady on the shoulder. "For somebody who's never been a cop, it's amazing you saw that at all."

Grady scoffed, but it was obvious he was fighting a smile. "There you go again, thinking the only person in the world with a brain has had to have police training somewhere along the line. Gillian, are you going to stand there and take that?"

"You're not talking about me," Gillian said. "My dad put me through a tougher course growing up than they face at the police academy."

"I should have known the two of you would stick together on this." He put the finishing touches on the first coat of drywall compound on his patch, then said, "Well, I can't stand around here all day yapping with you two, there's work to be done."

Seth said, "Did you have any luck outside?"

"Now what makes you think I had time to track our

shooter? I replaced your window, swept up the glass and fixed the drywall to boot."

Seth shook his head. "Sorry, I guess I should have known it was too much to expect."

Grady frowned. "Now what kind of comment is that? Of course I looked outside, that was the first thing I did at daybreak." He looked down at his hands for a moment. "I found an empty bottle of Boone's Farm wine and a few cigarette butts near the road, but somebody could have just decided to clean out his car and dumped that garbage right out on the ground. It's a miracle they didn't start a fire; it's been so dry around here lately that I doubt a herd of cattle would leave footprints. Sorry, whoever took those shots looks like a dead end."

Seth patted Grady on the shoulder. "Don't worry about it. We'll get them next time."

Grady offered a frightening grim smile. "Oh, you can bet the farm on that."

After he was gone, Gillian said, "You really think whoever shot at us will come back?"

"I don't plan on giving this up, do you? If there was malice in those shots, I imagine they might be willing to try again." After Gillian shook her head in disbelief, he added, "I didn't think so, though. They won't get past Grady next time, even if they do try again."

Seth heard a car approach on the gravel driveway and went to the door. Wonderful. It was the sheriff's personal car, and from the speed Kline was driving, Seth was sure the sheriff wasn't bringing him any good news.

He was right. Before Seth could say a word, Kline snapped, "I understand you're harboring fugitives now. Is she here at the house now, or do you have her tucked away somewhere?"

Seth kept his voice level and calm. "Afternoon, Sheriff. How are you doing?"

"You know how I'm doing, I'm pissed off. You want to explain to me what you think you're doing sticking your nose in my investigation? Last I heard you were retired, and unless Ruth down at the License Bureau is sleeping on the job, you haven't applied for a private investigator's license from the state of North Carolina, either. Where is she?"

Seth raised his hands. "I swear, I don't have the slightest idea. How'd you find out I talked to her, anyway?" He knew that Allison wouldn't have said anything, since she was in theory Penny's attorney. As for Gillian, she knew better, too. No, someone must have seen them all together. Was somebody watching Seth, or were they following Penny? Either way, it added a variable to an already confusing mix.

"You're not the only one in this town with his ear to the ground." In a hurt tone, he said, "Why didn't you come to me? You know I'd have done right by you."

"I tried to get Penny to turn herself in last night, I even found a lawyer to represent her, but she refused to budge until this morning."

Still steaming, he said, "Did you come in when I was out for breakfast, cause I sure don't have Penny in custody, and it's a shade past morning now."

Seth saw the sheriff's gaze go between Gillian and him to the interior of the cottage. He said, "Go ahead, search the place. I know you want to."

Kline nodded. "Thanks, I will."

One thing about the cottage, it was too small to hide anyone effectively. The sheriff lingered over Grady's drywall patches, touching the damp compound with a fingertip. "Doing a little remodeling?"

Keeping a straight face, Seth said, "You know how it is when you own your own home, there's always something around the place that needs fixing."

The Sheriff pointed to Gillian. "I suppose you've got the same explanation for this, too, don't you?"

"I'm trying to get him to paint. I think patching a few spots is a good place to start. I'm torn between Summer Sky Blue and Faded Rose. What do you think?"

"Frankly, I don't care if you paint it black and put in

black lights."

Kline stepped up to Seth and matched him toe to toe. The men's noses were two inches apart, but Seth didn't flinch. He'd used the same technique a thousand times. By invading someone's personal space, it was amazing how uncomfortable they would become. Instead of reacting by taking a step back, Seth nudged forward until he could feel the sheriff's breath on his chin. Kline gave it up, pulled away and turned to the door. Before he left, he said, "I could have you arrested for obstructing justice, you know that, don't you?"

Seth said, "I'm trying to help your investigation, not hinder it. I want Penny in custody just as much as you do. At least then I'll know she's safe."

Kline snapped, "I don't need any help, Seth, not now, not ever. I'm the elected sheriff around here. If you've got a problem with that, you're free to run next election day."

Seth knew the sheriff had a point. He himself would have been resentful if their roles were reversed. Whether Sheriff Kline realized it or not, the two men were on the same side. Trying to put some empathy in his voice, he said, "Sheriff, I give you my word as a former law enforcement officer that the next time I learn of Penny's whereabouts, I'll contact you immediately. As for the job, no thanks, you're welcome to it for as long as you want it, as far as I'm concerned."

That seemed to calm the sheriff somewhat. "Seth, you know how it is. I've got the mayor and most of the town council breathing down my neck to find her, and ninety percent of them are clamoring for me to call in the State Police. Blast it! I can handle this myself. I'm not on a witch-hunt. If this woman has a reasonable explanation for why her knife was found in the victim's chest, say an ironclad alibi or something like that, I'll start looking at other suspects. But I can't make that call until I can find her."

Seth nodded. "I'm really sorry, I expected her to be in your custody by now."

Kline shrugged, then slapped him on the shoulder. "Oh, crud. Sorry I snapped at you. It's just—"

Seth laughed gently. "Forget about it. I've been in your shoes before. I know how hot it can get."

Kline nodded. "Okay, I've got to go. I've got a meeting with the mayor in half an hour. I don't know how he expects me to solve any crimes if I spend most of my waking hours in meetings with him."

Kline tipped his head to Gillian, then drove off, this time at a much more sedate pace. Seth turned to Gillian. "You were awfully quiet the whole time he was here. You don't approve of my stance, do you? Gillian, he's got a job to do, a tough one at that. Besides, Harley Kline is a good cop. Once he talks to Penny, he'll have to acknowledge that there are other possibilities, but as long as she's a fugitive, he doesn't have any choice but to wonder about her."

Gillian shook her head. "It's not that, I'm beginning to think that you were right. I'm just amazed by how you just handled the sheriff."

"I didn't handle him. We just had a conversation."

"Don't take offense, it was a compliment. He came here ready to chew nails and spit lead, and by the time he left I swear I thought I heard him whistling. I wish I had your knack with people."

Seth shrugged her words off. "He just needed an outlet, and after I let him vent a little, I eased him out of it. It's not what I'd call a special talent."

"Nobody thinks their own talent is as good as the next person's. Trust me, what you've got is a gift for dealing with people in exactly the right way."

"Okay, I believe you. You've got a talent or two yourself, you know?"

"Such as?"

Seth hugged her gently. "No, I'm not going to tell you. You're just fishing for compliments." He loosened his grasp, then said, "We've lost most of the afternoon. How about an early dinner, then we can see if we can find Ace or Penny back at the spot we found them last night."

"I thought you wanted to interrogate more suspects?"

Seth shook his head. "We need to produce Penny; the rest can wait."

The Oak was a fine new restaurant, a place Seth and Gillian had already fallen in love with. Built as a timber-frame structure, massive beams were exposed to the interior diners offering a large open expanse inside that the owners had used to its full advantage. Honey toned wood covered the cathedral ceiling, and a central clerestory cupola let in segments of the sky. As they drove up, they could see the huge copper weathervane at the peak, a dancing oak leaf, turn as the wind touched it. The leaf motif was repeated throughout the restaurant itself, from the cocktail napkins to the subtle pattern of the tablecloth and the embossed menus. A massive fireplace structure was in the center of the dining room, sporting back to back hearths that offered realistic flickering flames from duel gas fireplaces. The fireplaces had fooled Seth initially; they were so realistic. He even heard the pops and crackles of wood burning. After some careful study, he saw a pinecone that didn't look quite real in back of the hearth. The manager confirmed his guess that the cone was in actuality a small powerful speaker, bouncing recorded noises off the back of the bricks and sending them into the dining room.

The walls of the restaurant were adorned with some Bob Timberlake originals, and Seth recognized that the structure itself had been inspired by Timberlake's own showplace in the North Carolina town of Lexington. Seth was a huge fan of the realist artist who had made a name for himself all over the world. He even had a print of a snow-covered well on the wall of his cottage. Above, a collection of white ceiling fans thirty feet above the floor lazily spun, circulating the warm air from the peak back down to the diners.

Every table at The Oak was taken when Seth and Gillian arrived, so they decided to go to the bar while they waited with a couple of drinks. The bar was an intimate space tucked under one eave of the structure, its colors and tones purposely drawn down to dusk. Soft Celtic music played in the background, and Seth found his mood relaxing into the atmosphere.

"What do you feel like drinking?" he asked Gillian. They'd gone back to her place so she could change, and in less than twenty minutes she had transformed herself from an ordinary woman into a striking lady. She wore a red dress cut just above the knee that looked as if it had been designed with only her in mind. Skillfully applied makeup looked as if she was wearing none at all. Seth completely understood the eyes of approval she brought from the bar's other patrons. He was satisfied to wear a gray suit, his only splash of color a burgundy tie that matched the shade of Gillian's dress perfectly. He wondered briefly if she'd chosen that particular dress just to coordinate with him.

She said, "Maybe we'd better stick to wine tonight if we're going to be working later."

"Now what fun is that?"

Gillian smiled, then told the bartender, "Two white wines, please."

As they collected their glasses, Seth steered Gillian to a small table that offered a spectacular view of the Tacawba river. It was lovely, especially at night. A few intrepid boaters were out on the water, and their identifying lights echoed ripples of muted brilliance off the dancing water of their wakes.

As Seth was enjoying the music and the view, he heard a disturbance at the end of the bar. A man dressed in a disheveled suit had started muttering to himself, and the decibel level of his soliloquy had steadily grown until it was encroaching on nearby drinkers. As he turned on his stool, Seth saw that it was Kevin Garska, one of the town councilmen. Garska kept repeating, "It's not fair, it's just not fair."

Seth saw the bartender approach and speak softly to

Garska. His words had no effect on the outbursts, which were rapidly escalating in volume. "Vera's gone, I'm telling you. Don't you understand?"

Seth felt the hair on the back of his neck quiver. He motioned to Gillian to stay where she was and walked quickly over to the drunken man. The bartender was saying, "Mr. Garska, if you can't keep your voice down, I'm going to have to ask you to leave."

Seth put a strong hand on the drinker's shoulder and said, "I think we both need some fresh air." His arm shifted to Garska's biceps, and Seth walked him to the door as a look of obvious relief spread across the bartender's face. Seth said softly to him, "Is he by himself tonight?" The bartender nodded, and Seth said, "Call a cab. We'll be outside waiting for it." Seth looked back at Gillian, held up a lone finger indicating he wouldn't be long, then walked the councilman outside. A row of benches under the generous wooden porch were free because of the brisk May wind, so they had no trouble finding a place to sit.

Garska stumbled as Seth guided him to the bench. "Take it easy, buddy."

"You don't understand. Vera's dead."

"Did you know her well?"

Garska put his hands in his head. "Yesterday morning she was here, and now she's gone."

Seth had interviewed plenty of drunks before. He knew if he kept patiently asking his questions, sooner or later he'd most likely get an answer. "I didn't realize you two were so close."

"Friends. We were friends." Garska lifted his head, stared at Seth, and added, "Oh boy, were we friends."

"Are you friends with Bradley, too?"

"Not a chance. He wasn't good enough for her."

"But you were," Seth said softly.

"You got that right. We belonged together. We dated all through high school, but we had a fight. Terrible fight. None of them ever loved her, not like I did."

"When was the last time you saw her, Garska?"

It didn't appear that Garska heard the question as he rambled on, "Bradley's a real piece of work. He's probably over at Sandi's house now, the son of a dog. Who ever heard of spelling Sandi with an 'i', I ask you that."

"Who's Sandi?"

Garska snapped churlishly, "Haven't you been listening? Vera's dead, and Bradley's with his girlfriend. I told Vera to let him go, he wasn't worth the trouble, but she wouldn't do it, said she had too much pride to admit she'd made another mistake. Now she's dead." The man started whimpering softly, he was feeling real pain. Seth tried to bring him out, to distract him with a few questions, but the councilman was lost in his own private grief. At last, the taxi showed up and Seth helped Garska into the back. The cab driver said, "Where to?" and Seth waited there long enough to hear Garska give him an address. He hoped it was the right one.

Seth flipped a twenty in the cabby's lap and said, "Make sure he gets inside, will you?"

The cab driver tucked the bill in his shirt pocket and said, "For an extra twenty I'll even tuck him in."

Gillian wasn't at the small table in the bar where he'd left her. The bartender said, "She's already been seated in the main dining area. Thanks for taking care of him. We don't get many rowdy drunks in here, at least not town councilmen."

Seth said, "No problem."

As he found Gillian, she couldn't wait to question him. "What was that all about?"

"It seems Garska and Vera were high school sweethearts. He claims that they've stayed friends through the years, and I caught a distinct impression that they were more than just casual acquaintances."

Gillian whispered, "Do you think they were having an affair? Vera? I don't believe it."

"I don't either, not that I think Garska wouldn't have

jumped at the chance. If what he told me is true though, the same can't be said for Bradley. The councilman kept mentioning some woman named Sandi with an 'i.'"

Gillian frowned. "Sandi? You're kidding."

"You know her?"

"It can't be the same person I'm thinking of. There's a girl who helps me out sometimes at Brightman's department store, but she's only eighteen or nineteen. I'd say Bradley's a little old for her."

Seth shrugged. "Maybe not. Some men get hung up on eighteen-year-old girls when they're teenagers, and they never get over the fascination."

Gillian patted his hand. "I'm so glad you're not one of them." Gillian drank the last of her wine, then suddenly put her glass down. "It's her, I know it."

"What are you talking about?"

"Remember when we were at Bradley's house and I hit redial? That's who was on the other end of the line, it was Sandi Ingalls."

"Are you sure?"

"Yes, it was just hearing her voice in a different context that threw me. It was Sandi, there's no doubt in my mind."

Seth took a sip of wine, then said, "I want to get more information from Garska, preferably when he's sober. After we know more, it'll be time to tackle Sandi."

The waiter approached and asked them if they were ready to order.

Without looking at the menu, Gillian said, "I'll have the Trout Almandine, house salad, and another white wine."

Seth ordered a steak, and after the waiter was gone, he said, "I love this place. It feels like home."

Gillian said, "Admit it, Seth, you wouldn't live in a place this size if the owners offered it to you free and clear. You like well-defined space around you."

He shrugged. "I guess that's true, but it's still a marvelous place."

Desiree Young, the owner of The Oak, came to their table

with the slight crease of a frown on her face. "Good evening Mr. Jackson, Ms. Graywolf. I understand there was a bit of a disturbance in the bar tonight. I was in the kitchen dealing with a temperamental chef, but I've been informed you handled the situation admirably."

Seth bowed his head slightly. "It was nothing, I was glad I could help."

"Please, you are too modest. Allow me to pick up your check tonight. Dinner is on The Oak."

"Ms. Young, that's really not necessary."

She held a hand up, instantly dismissing his protest. "I insist. Enjoy your evening with my thanks." With that she was gone.

Seth played with his fork a minute, and Gillian said, "It makes you uncomfortable accepting things from people, doesn't it?"

"My motives weren't exactly altruistic. I wanted to hear what Garska had to say about Vera, and I figured the only way I could do that was by getting him away from everyone else."

"Even if he hadn't said a word about Vera, you would have stepped in, anyway, admit it. You're good at defusing situations, why shouldn't you?"

"Okay, so I helped out a little. A free meal seems a little bit of an overreaction, doesn't it?"

She patted his hand across the table. "Just enjoy the gesture, okay?"

"You don't have any problem with accepting it?"

Gillian laughed. "Are you kidding? I'm even going to order dessert. Chocolate Mousse sounds good to me."

"Okay, I'm convinced. Just don't eat too much. We've got to change into something a little less glamorous after dinner and see if we can track Penny and Ace down."

"What better reason to add some calories we're just going to walk off tonight anyway?" She paused, and the lightness of her tone faded away for a moment. "They'll turn up, Seth, don't worry. Let's just enjoy our meal."

The food was excellent, especially the dessert, but as they left the restaurant the chill wind stole the warm glow of their evening. Seth wanted to find Ace and Penny, and he was determined to find them quickly.

Chapter 10

As they drove downtown after changing clothes, Gillian watched Seth and thought about the alterations he'd brought into her life. She'd always considered herself a woman in charge of her own destiny, never feeling that she needed a man in her world to be complete. Granted, they could be awfully nice to have around, but necessary to her existence? Hardly. She'd managed to retain her independence throughout a bad marriage and the carnage she'd managed of dating before and after. All of that was before Seth. From the instant they'd met, she knew that there would be none of the usual games and posturing men and women played. He had an open, honest 'This is the way I am' attitude that had struck a similar cord in her heart. He wasn't afraid to be himself, and she'd found that refreshing, not to mention intriguing.

He looked over at her and said, "You're suddenly very quiet. What are you thinking?"

"Oh, just letting my mind drift."

He smiled softly and said, "Well, it's time to bring it in to shore. We're here," as he pulled into a row of empty parking spaces. Waist-high silver poles stood at each lined spot on the curb, headless sentinels in the night. Gillian had heard that the town of Jackson's Ferry had abandoned the idea of charging parking fees after the fifth or sixth time vandals knocked the meters to the ground and broke them open for pitifully small handfuls of change.

As they got out, she was glad she'd added her heavy flannel jacket to her outfit. It had been her father's, and she always felt safe wearing it. Having Seth beside her didn't hurt, either. No matter what else he was to her, Gillian knew Seth was a good man to have at her side if there was the potential for trouble.

Seth reached behind the seat and took out a four-cell

metal flashlight. "Do we really need all that light?" she asked.

He tapped it gently into his free palm. "It doubles as a night stick, too."

"I thought you brought your gun," she said in soft voice. Seth tapped the pocket of his large gray jacket. "Don't worry, I've got it right here. Sometimes though, it's better not to show all the cards you're holding. Chances are this flashlight will be enough, even if we run into a spot of trouble."

Gillian said, "Aren't you worried about your truck?"

He patted it affectionately. "Spot can take care of herself. Besides, who'd want to steal her?" He'd named his truck 'Spot' since it sported several spots of gray primer over the areas where the original blue paint had peeled. It was his way, having fun with the fact that he chose not to spend the money for a paint job he felt unnecessary. He didn't apologize for not having a lot of money; sometimes it seemed to Gillian that he reveled in it, showing the world that outward signs of wealth just didn't matter all that much to him.

As they walked toward the place they'd left Ace and Penny the night before, Gillian put her arm in Seth's. He looked at her and said, "Getting cold?"

"No, I just thought we were out for a romantic walk under the stars." Streetlights, those that hadn't been broken out with rocks, obliterated any possible light from the sky.

He freed his arm and wrapped it around her shoulders. "Do I know how to show a lady a good time, or what?"

"Sometimes it leaves me breathless."

"I think that's just the cold." He cut off the light and said, "Somebody's up ahead in the shadows. Make that two people. Stay right beside me."

Gillian nodded as they walked. Instead of the route they'd been taking, Seth moved directly toward the shadows. In a clear voice that cut the darkness, he said, "Kind of cold out tonight, isn't it?"

After a brief whispering, the two forms stepped out of the shadows. Two men Gillian had never seen before were impatient and tense, each with a club-length of wood in their hands.

The taller of the two men said, "Kind of risky, walking around down here without any protection. Aren't you afraid your girlfriend's going to get hurt?"

Though Seth feigned a laugh, Gillian saw his free hand slip into his jacket. "You don't know what you're talking about, she's protecting me." Suddenly, the levity was gone from his voice. "I wouldn't recommend trying anything, boys. You'll regret it, I promise you."

The bigger of the two men spat on the ground near Seth's feet. "I don't remember asking you for your opinion."

Seth nudged the gun forward in the fold of jacket. The other thug caught the movement and realized its implication immediately. Abruptly, he said, "Come on, Buck, quit picking on the man."

In a lower voice, Buck turned on his partner and said, "What's wrong with you, Spider, we agreed--."

Spider said, "You're on your own then," and hurried down an alley behind them, his eyes never leaving Seth's.

Buck looked at Seth and Gillian a second before saying, "I guess it's your lucky night," before turning to go.

Seth said, "I'd have to say your friend made the right choice. We're not the only lucky ones tonight."

There was a hitch as Buck stopped walking away, and Gillian worried that Seth might have pushed him too far. Buck smiled, showing a row of bad teeth common to the area and said, "Another time, then?"

"I can hardly wait."

With that, the man was gone.

Gillian said, "That was close. I was afraid you'd goaded him too much at the end."

"Buck wasn't the problem, it was Spider I was worried about. He had a gun himself, I could see it bulging in his coat, and it was pointing right at us. Otherwise I never would have let them know I was armed. We had a stand-off for a second, and Spider must have decided a mugging wasn't worth getting shot over. Once he was gone, I knew we wouldn't have any more trouble with Buck."

One block away, Seth said, "Here's where we saw Ace and Penny last night. Let me go in first. I want you to keep your eyes on our backs once we get inside the pallets. If you hear or see anything suspicious, touch my shoulder and I'll stop. Anything at all, Gillian, okay?"

She nodded and they started in. As Seth crept into the space, she saw a light at the far end. In a few seconds, they were inside.

The grotto wasn't empty anymore.

At least Ace had made it back.

But he was alone.

Ace's expression of hope dropped the second he saw it was them. "I thought you were Penny."

Seth asked roughly, "What happened to you two, Ace? We were supposed to see the lawyer this morning, or did you have a more pressing appointment somewhere else?"

"Don't get mad at me, Seth, it's not my fault. Penny seemed fine with the idea last night, but sometime in the middle of the night she must have changed her mind. I woke up around six this morning and she was gone."

Gillian asked, "She didn't leave you a note or anything?"

"Penny's got a lot of problems in this world, and one of them is that she can't read or write. When I found out she was gone, I started searching all the places she might go. But like I told you before, she's a lot better at hiding than I am. I've been asking around, and nobody would admit to seeing her. Finally I gave up looking and headed back here for the night. I've been hoping she'd show up, but so far, no luck."

"The police are getting impatient," Seth said sternly.

"You don't have to tell me. They've been making my search that much harder. You can't turn around down here without bumping into a couple of cops. They're searching in pairs, did you know that? I guess they're afraid a few of us bums will gang up on them. Penny better turn herself in pretty soon, some of the questioning is starting to get a little rough. I don't want any of our people to start having 'accidents' while the police question them."

Gillian said, "Come on, Ace, aren't you exaggerating? Cops beating witnesses went out with moonshine stills."

"If you know where to ask, you can still get a quart jar of moonshine in Jackson's Ferry for five bucks. The police might be politically correct when they're dealing with taxpayers, but we don't exactly inspire the fear of lawsuits in them. I'm not saying all the cops in Jackson's Ferry are bad, there are three or four I'm even friends with, but there always seems to be a bad apple or two in the barrel no matter where you're at."

With an edge of steel in his voice, Seth said, "Well it's not going to happen around here. If you hear anything from someone you consider credible, come to me with names and I'll make sure it doesn't happen again."

"Nobody I know is what you'd call good on the witness stand."

Gillian heard the silent fury in Seth's voice as he said, "Who said anything about a trial? You know who can be believed and who can't. Sheriff Kline and I might not see eye to eye on modern law enforcement techniques, but he's a good man. I know he won't tolerate that kind of behavior on his force."

Ace nodded with new respect in the way he looked at Seth. "I'll keep my eyes open. Thanks, Seth."

"Nothing to thank me for. We don't need any bullies on the police force." He took a deep breath, then said, "That doesn't bring us any closer to finding Penny. Do you have any idea where she might be hiding?"

Ace hung his head low. "I swear to you, I've looked everywhere I can think of. She's just not here."

Gillian said, "Maybe she's not downtown at all. Don't some people stay down by the river? I've heard there are a few makeshift shacks down there."

Ace shook his head. "In the summertime maybe, but when the cold breeze comes off the water it's freezing down there; believe me, I know. Anyway, you wouldn't find Penny down there if it was the Fourth of July. She hates the water. She won't even take a bath or a shower at the shelter. The most I've ever seen her do is take a sponge bath, and those are rare enough as it is."

Seth said, "So what are we supposed to do? The longer Penny waits to turn herself in, the harsher the cops are going to treat her. I'm afraid she's just making things worse for herself by hiding."

"That's why I'm here. I'll let you know when she gets back, I promise."

Gillian reached into her purse and pulled out her cellular phone. She dialed her own number quickly, waiting to make sure her answering machine kicked in, then shut off the telephone and handed it to Ace. "Don't try to find a pay phone, just hit redial. It'll ring my loft."

Ace looked at the phone without touching it. "You trust me with that thing? It's got to be worth at least a few bucks."

"You thinking about hocking it?"

"No, of course not."

Gillian shrugged. "So what's the problem? Once you get Penny, I don't want to take a chance on losing her again."

Ace nodded as he accepted the telephone. "Thanks."

She smiled warmly, then turned to Seth. "Why don't we go and let Ace get some rest. It's hard to tell when Penny's going to show up, and when she does, he needs to be alert."

Seth agreed. As they were leaving, he said, "Ace, it doesn't matter what time it is, if Penny shows up, we want you to call us."

"Are you going to be staying at Gillian's?" He paused a moment, then added, "I'm not being nosy, it's just that I'd feel better if you were closer to town. If you're out at your farm, it's going to add fifteen minutes to your time getting here, and to be honest with you, I'm not sure I can get Penny to hang around that long."

Before Seth could answer, Gillian said, "He'll be close by, don't worry."

After saying goodnight, they walked back to the truck. Seth said, "I'm beginning to think there's a conspiracy keeping me from my house at night."

"What's the matter, are you getting tired of being my houseguest?"

"You know that's not it. Your place is just too big for me, Gillian. I like to have the roof over my head a lot closer than it is at your place."

She said, "You can put your head under the covers, if that will help."

"If my head's under the covers, I won't be sleeping."

"All the better, then."

He laughed. "You're incorrigible, you know that, don't you?"

"It's part of my charm, don't you think?"

He stopped and kissed her there on the street. After pulling away, he whispered in her ear, "I couldn't agree with you more."

The next morning, Seth and Gillian were nearing Kevin Garska's house when she said, "I still think we should call before we just pop in on him. He was in pretty bad shape at The Oak last night."

"That's precisely why we're disturbing him so early. I don't want him to have a chance to pull himself together before we talk to him. Besides, we have a perfect excuse for being there. We can tell him we wanted to make sure he got home all right last night."

Gillian asked, "Should we call Ace first before we tackle the councilman?"

Seth patted her hand. "He would have called us if he'd found her. Give him some time, he'll track her down." As he parked in front of Garska's house, there wasn't a sign of life inside. "Looks like he might still be asleep. All the better for us."

At Garska's doorstep, Gillian's finger hesitated over the doorbell. "Nothing in the world like being jerked out of your sleep with a hangover and the doorbell ringing."

Seth smiled. He said, "You're absolutely right," then proceeded to bang on the doorframe with his fists, rattling it in its frame.

Kevin Garska came to the door surprisingly fast. He was dressed in a somber gray suit and his hair was neatly combed, but his bleary eyes and the pallor of his skin betrayed his condition.

In a voice Gillian suspected was purposely a little too loud, Seth said, "Good, you made it home last night. I was worried about you when I poured you into that cab."

Garska held his hands up, as if trying to defend himself from the volume. In a much softer voice, he said, "I thought I remembered seeing you at The Oak last night. Thanks for your help." There was a tone of dismissal in his voice, but Gillian wasn't surprised when Seth failed to respond.

He said, "Is that coffee I smell? I sure would love some to take the chill off the morning."

Garska reluctantly nodded as he stepped aside. Hangover or not, he had too much Southern manners to refuse the obvious request. "Come on in."

Seth walked past him, and Gillian followed, offering a sympathetic look as she entered the house. It had been fairly obvious that the city councilman wasn't used to drinking from his behavior the night before, and she knew he must be having a whale of a morning after. Still, she had to remember that the main part of her sympathy had to be held in reserve for Vera.

Garska's home was obviously a place where a man lived alone, though not in Seth's style. Both houses were neat enough, though Seth could learn a thing or two from the councilman on orderliness. No, it was more a feel, a texture to the space that betrayed the lack of a woman's presence. Seth's house had the same feel to it, though they were decorated completely differently. Where Seth loved pieces with simple, Shaker-style lines, Garska had Victorian furniture sporting ornate carvings and moldings. He saw her looking around and said, "These pieces aren't exactly my taste, but they've been in my family for generations. Sometimes I feel like they're more a part of Garska history than I am."

After they were both served steaming cups of aromatic coffee, they moved into the living room. Gillian took a tentative sip and recoiled. The brew was so strong, she was amazed the porcelain mug didn't crumble. Garska noticed her reaction.

"Sorry it's a little lively, but I needed it. I'm not used to drinking, I don't know what came over me."

Gillian said, "You don't have to apologize. When someone close to you dies, it's hard to deal with. You're entitled to a little excess in your mourning."

Garska nodded, and immediately regretted the disturbance. As he rubbed his temples, he said, "It's nice of you to say so. Yes, Vera and I were close." He looked embarrassed as he asked, "What exactly did I say last night?"

Seth said, "You don't remember?"

"It's pretty much a blur after my second drink at the bar. I'm afraid I've never held my liquor well, I've got a low tolerance for the stuff. I can get drunk on two drinks that a normal man my size would hardly feel." He rubbed his forehead. "Believe me, I felt them last night. I'm still feeling them."

Gillian nodded, trying to look as sympathetic as she could. "Could you tell us about Vera, how you knew her? Seth and I volunteered with her at the Soup Kitchen and once on a Habitat for Humanity house, but we didn't know her nearly as well as you did."

Garska leaned back in his chair, and it seemed to Gillian that the mention of Vera's name had momentarily taken the sting out of his hangover. "You didn't know Vera when she was younger. When we were in school, every boy in three grades was after her. She chose me," he said proudly. "We dated two years and planned to get married as soon as we finished college. I went away the summer after we graduated high school to work on my uncle's dairy farm. It was the only way I could afford the tuition. I came back home two months later and learned that Vera had married Jared Skyles. She was showing even then, pregnant with Jason. The guy was six years older than we were, and he was a real hellion, not Vera's type at all. I didn't talk to her for four years, and when I came home from school on breaks I managed to find excuses to avoid her, and let me tell you, Jackson's Ferry's small enough to make that tough. I heard a rumor about Jared running off my sophomore year, and I thought about calling her even though she'd broken my heart. But by the time I got the chance, she was already seeing Bradley Hobart, and it was too late for us again. They got married when I was a junior, and that was that. The last thing in the world I wanted to do was come back home after I graduated, but my dad got sick, so I promised I'd help him out with his insurance company until he got back on his feet again. Three weeks later he died, and I had to run the business myself." He took a sip of his coffee. "I could have sold it to another agent, in fact I'd decided to do just that. But at Dad's funeral, Vera came over here and I couldn't avoid her any longer. She begged my forgiveness for betraying me, and told me that she really had loved me, but she was with Hobart now. We patched up our differences on the spot, mainly because I realized if I couldn't have her for my wife, at least I could have her for a friend." He looked at Seth and said, "It sounds pretty pathetic when I say it out loud like that, doesn't it?"

Seth shook his head. "I know how much it can hurt to lose someone you love. It had to be tough, just being friends."

Garska laughed. "You'd think so, but we both adapted right into the role. Hobart didn't seem to mind. He struck me as a good enough fellow at first, but there always seemed to be some resentment between him and Jason. I did more with the boy than Hobart ever did. Jason never was what you'd call a pleasant kid, and the older he got, the meaner he became. Finally, even Vera gave up on him, though the two of them had gotten close again in the last few months." He shook his head slightly, then remembered his hangover.

Gillian asked, "What brought on the change of heart?"

"I don't guess it'll hurt to say anything, it'll be public knowledge soon enough. You know Vera and Hobart were finally splitting up. She and I were going to try to make things work between us, at least we'd been talking about it. But Vera wanted to make sure Jason knew she still loved him the most of anyone in her life, so without telling Hobart, she quietly switched beneficiaries in her will from Hobart to Jason last month."

Seth asked, "Is much money involved?"

"The policy was written for two million dollars. I can't wait to see Hobart's face when I tell him he's not getting a dime."

Gillian asked, "Did Jason know about the change in the policy?"

"I can't say for sure, but it wouldn't surprise me a bit. I guess he'll be able to quit that welding he does and live a normal life now."

Gillian said, "He really is talented, you know. I've seen several of his pieces."

"I'll have to take your word for it, I don't know much about art, or what goes for art nowadays. I'm a numbers man, I guess I always have been." He looked at his watch and stood up, just a little too quickly. Gillian saw him clutch the side of his chair a moment as he quelled his nausea. He said, "Like it or not, I've got to get to my office. I've got three clients scheduled for this morning, and I'm already late. I've got to be at the funeral, it's at two, and then there's a wake afterward at The Clusters. There's going to be at least one person there who really loved her, I can guarantee you that."

As the three of them made their way to the door, Garska said, "Now where did I put my car? That's right, I took a cab home last night."

"We can give you a ride to your office, we're going that way anyway."

It was obvious Garska wanted to turn them down, but it was equally apparent he didn't have much choice. Reluctantly, he said, "Thanks, just let me get my briefcase."

Two minutes later they were in the truck heading to the respectable section of Jackson's Ferry's business district. As he drove, Seth asked, "How did Vera really feel about Hobart leaving? She had to be disillusioned, having two husbands run out on her."

"Skyles ran, it was more like Hobart was limping away. At first, Vera denied the marriage was breaking up. She wouldn't give him a divorce no matter how many times he asked. You want to know the honest truth? In the end, I think she was as ready to shed him as he was to get rid of her. That's the worst part about this mess, she lost out on one last chance to be happy."

Gillian smiled gently at him. "You did, too."

He nodded, and for a moment she thought he might start crying. As they let him off in front of his office, he said, "I appreciate you two listening to me ramble. It helped, talking about her. Are you going to be at the funeral?"

Seth said, "We'll be there, you can count on it."

"Good. See you then."

After he was gone, Gillian said, "We're going to the funeral?"

"As a cop, I never missed one. You never know what you're going to see, but it's always worth a chance."

Gillian spotted a pay phone on the corner. "Stay right here, I need to make a call."

Seth handed her some change. "You're going to check up on Ace, aren't you?"

"I just want to see how he's doing."

She could feel Seth's gaze on her as she walked away,

and could imagine him shaking his head.

Chapter 11

Seth sat in the truck as Gillian made her call. He figured it was a waste of time, she'd already checked her answering machine and hadn't found a single message. Ace would have telephoned if he'd found out anything, but there was no sense arguing with Gillian about it. He knew she'd call anyway, and he'd learned it was best to just let the little things ride. Besides, they had plenty of time before they had to be at Vera's funeral. Seth hated funerals, and had refused to attend a single one since he'd buried Melissa. The event had turned him off funerals forever, and he'd already left specific instructions with his attorney that he was to be cremated as soon as possible and his ashes scattered over the Christmas tree farm. It helped him, feeling that his remains would go on as a part of other people's celebrations for years to come. He'd never mentioned his plans to Gillian, and decided he should bring it up so she wouldn't be caught off guard if something should suddenly happen to him.

Gillian came back to the truck with her lips set into a grim line.

Seth asked, "Something wrong?"

"You were right, he hasn't found her yet."

"It was worth a try."

Gillian looked at her watch. "We've got some time to kill before the funeral."

Seth said, "And I know just how to fill it. I think it's time we paid a visit to Sandi Ingalls."

"She's not going to tell us anything, Seth. This 'concerned friend' front we're presenting won't do us any good with Sandi. She's probably celebrating Vera's death if she wanted to get her hooks into Hobart."

Seth smiled. "That's why we didn't go see her first. She could brush us off if we went by her apartment, but she's most likely at work by now. Do you think she's going to be able to blow us off if we stand at her counter in cosmetics and keep asking her questions? She might think Hobart's going to marry her, but she's bound to be shrewd enough not to lose her job until she's certain."

"He wouldn't be the first married man who promised to leave his wife when he didn't mean it. I never thought of that, but Hobart might have considered Vera more of a convenience to his love life than a hindrance."

Seth shook his head. "We do have corroborating evidence that they were splitting up. Vera told Lex and Garska, and Hobart didn't deny it himself."

As Seth parked in front of Brightman's department store, he said, "Let's see what Sandi has to say."

They found her working at the counter, an array of cosmetics and perfume displayed in front of her. She was a slender young woman with artificially blonde hair and in Seth's opinion, Sandi wore way too much makeup. He found her choice of dresses for the day interesting, to say the least. Though the outfit was cut well up the thigh, at least it was the deep black of mourning color.

When she saw them approach, she offered a chipper smile. "Good morning, welcome to Brightman's. Hi, Gillian."

Seth said, "You're wearing black. Don't tell me you're actually going to the funeral."

Sandi's smile disappeared. "I knew Vera, why shouldn't I be there?"

Gillian picked up on Seth's cue. "Oh, I'd say sleeping with Hobart would be reason enough to stay away from his wife's funeral, but maybe I'm just old fashioned."

Sandi's face reddened. "I don't know who's spreading those wicked rumors, but Bradley Hobart and I are not sleeping together."

"You're just friends, is that it?"

"He needed someone to talk to, and I was willing to listen. Is that wrong, offering comfort to another human being?"

Gillian said, "It depends on what kind of comfort you were offering."

Sandi hissed, "Lower your voice, I'm working right now, I don't have time to talk to you."

Gillian picked up a bottle of Obsession and said, "Now is that any way to speak to your customers? Perhaps I should get your manager over here."

Sandi glanced over her shoulder as she said, "Okay, you win. I can't afford to leave this job, not until I'm ready." She pointed to the bottle of perfume. "You're at least going to buy that if I'm answering questions."

Seth said, "Let's just see how well you answer questions first."

Petulantly, she asked, "What exactly is it you want to know?"

Gillian placed the glass back on the counter. "Were you sleeping with Bradley Hobart, yes or no?"

After a moment's hesitation, she nodded. "Okay, I admit it. Now will you leave me alone?"

Seth said, "Not yet, but you're doing fine so far. Where were you two days ago around noon?"

"You think I killed her? You're crazy, I was right here working my counter. I didn't want her dead, Bradley told me he'd have his freedom soon. Now why would I wish any harm to that woman? I already had her husband."

Seth saw a dark suited man approaching. He had the officious look of a supervisor in his eyes and gait. Before he could get there, Seth said, "Do you think Hobart could have killed her?"

"Bradley? He was getting a divorce, there was no reason to do anything that drastic."

As the manager's footsteps approached, Seth said, "If I were you, I'd watch my step. What if Hobart did kill her? Things like that run in patterns, and you don't want it to happen again when he finds a replacement for you."

Before Sandi could say a word of protest, the man arrived. "Is there a problem here?"

Gillian smiled sweetly, then said, "We were considering a perfume purchase, but we've changed our minds. Your young lady has been most helpful, though."

"Glad we could be of service to you." He was going to say something else when a voice over the store intercom paged him. "If you'll excuse me?"

Seth nodded. "Of course. We were just leaving ourselves."

After he was out of hearing range, Sandi snapped, "I thought you were going to buy some perfume."

Seth said, "I forgot to tell you, I'm allergic to the stuff. Sorry."

As Seth and Gillian walked outside, Seth said, "Do you believe her?"

Gillian thought about it a moment, then said, "I'm not saying she's telling the truth, but I think she believes everything she's saying. I also think she's hiding something, but I can't for the life of me figure out what it is. There's something that bothers me about her."

"Sleeping with Vera's husband isn't enough?"

"That's not what I'm talking about." After a pause for thought, she added, "I wonder when she took her lunch break the day Vera was murdered? We're not that far from downtown, and she'd certainly be able to disguise her appearance with enough makeup. We need a motive, though."

"Greed's my best bet. Divorced, Hobart would lose half of everything he owned. Widowed, he gets to keep all of his stuff, plus he probably thinks he's getting a million dollars kicked in for good measure. Sandi could have seen the opportunity for making a big score slip away, so she decided to kill Vera before the divorce. The same motive works for Hobart, too. Maybe he did it just for the aggravation she'd been causing him. He could have considered the insurance an added bonus for his years of service, unfaithful or otherwise."

"But he's not going to see a dime of that money, Garska

told us that himself."

Seth tapped the steering wheel. "Yeah, but did Hobart know that? Garska didn't seem to think so."

"Do you think there's a chance Jason killed his mother for the money?"

Seth stared out the window for a few seconds, then said, "You saw how he lives. A million dollars would buy a fully equipped studio with enough left over to live on comfortably for years. He admitted to us himself that the two of them had been estranged for a long time. Jason could have persuaded Vera to change her insurance, then kill her the first chance he got. It's happened before."

Seth saw a shiver go through Gillian. She was so astute, so observant that he had difficulty sometimes remembering that she'd never actually been a cop herself. Her father had trained her well, but she didn't have that final hardened edge of dealing with the crime he'd seen every day. It left her with a more positive outlook on life than he'd been able to muster, and the blend of her experience and innocence made her that much more attractive to him.

"I thought I knew Vera as well as could be expected, but there was this whole substratum to her life that I never even suspected. I didn't know her at all, not really, and now I'll never have the chance."

Seth said, "Somebody once told me that life was nothing more than a series of lost opportunities, but I don't believe it. Nobody can save the world, no matter how good their intentions are. We just have to do the best we can with what we've got, ease some of the pain and suffering we find, and make time to have some of the joy of life ourselves."

"You'd better watch yourself," Gillian said gently. "If you go around talking like that, people are going to think you're a philosopher, not an ex-cop."

"You'll keep my secret for me, won't you?"

"It's safe with me. Let's go get some lunch at Carston's. I think we should figure out what we've got so far before we tackle the funeral."

"That sounds like a plan to me."

After finishing their potato soup and club sandwiches at the small diner, Gillian pulled a notebook out of her purse. "Now let's see what we've got. Hobart has to go on the top of our list. We know he's got a motive, what else do we need?"

Seth pushed away his tea glass. "Just about anybody could have the means, it wasn't as if Penny's knife was under lock and key. That leaves opportunity. Does Hobart have an alibi at the time of the murder? We need to find out."

Gillian made a note, then said, "Jason Skyles is next. The same goes for him. He claims he was at his studio, and I don't see how we're going to be able to prove or disprove that. If he knew he was getting the money, a million dollars is all the motive he needs. What about Sandi?"

Seth motioned for a refill of his tea, then said, "She could be the greedy one, if she didn't want Hobart to start their new life together with half his money."

Gillian said, "To be honest with you, I'm beginning to have doubts about her. Do you really think that waif would have the strength to drive a knife into anyone's chest? She probably needs help carving the turkey at Thanksgiving, I doubt she weighs a hundred pounds."

"It's easier than you'd think. I've got to admit, though, she wouldn't exactly blend in with the street people we know, and I doubt anyone would mistake her for a volunteer."

"That part's easy. She works in cosmetics, it wouldn't be too difficult for her to make herself look indigent. Hide that little body of hers in some Salvation Army clothes and I'd bet most people wouldn't have a clue as to who was hiding underneath."

"She belongs on your list. That gives us three suspects so far. Put Garska down, too."

"The long lost boyfriend? Seth, he loved her, I could see it in his eyes when we spoke to him today."

After the waitress topped off their glasses with fresh tea, he said, "That's the problem. What if he loved her so much he wasn't willing for anyone else to have her? There's more than one explanation for his little drinking exhibition at The Oak last night. What if he was drinking out of guilt instead of out of loss? He could have been trying to drown his conscience if he killed her himself."

"Kevin Garska killing Vera in a jealous rage over unrequited love? I have a hard time seeing it."

"All I'm saying is that we can't ignore the possibility."

Gillian dutifully wrote Garska's name on her list, then said lightly, "If we're on a witch hunt, why don't we put Lex and her ex-husband's name on here, too? As neighbors, they might have been more embroiled in Vera's life than we know."

"I would like to know if Lex told us the truth about why her marriage is breaking up." Seth tapped the side of his glass with his spoon. "When we came back out of Hobart's house, she seemed awfully eager to share bad news with us."

Gillian laughed. "Seth, I'm beginning to think you're paranoid. You'll be suspecting the mailman next."

"It comes with the territory of being a cop. At the moment, I suspect everyone who's touched Vera's life, Penny included."

"But we know Penny had an aversion to killing anything, even an ant on the sidewalk. There's no way she could kill a person, especially not one who helped her."

"For all I know Penny believes in reincarnation and she was just helping Vera along to her next stop in the cosmos. She'd better turn up soon, or it's not going to matter what we find in our investigation." Seth held up a hand as he saw the sheriff's patrol car pull up out front. "It's Kline. Why don't you tuck that notebook back in your purse?"

The sheriff walked in and stood in front of their booth. "You're never far from your truck, are you, Seth?"

"What's up?"

"Just thought you'd like to know. We finally got an ID

on this Penny woman. Her real name's Ruby Parkinson. Turns out she's spent quite a bit of time at the Brolin Mental Institution. Figured you ought to know."

He walked over to the counter, ordered a cup of coffee to go, then left with a distinct smile on his face.

After he was gone, Gillian said, "Half the people we serve at the soup kitchen have been inside Brolin, it doesn't prove anything."

"She was unstable enough to be committed to a mental institution. That won't help her case any."

Gillian said, "Then we'll just have to work harder to prove she's innocent."

As Seth paid the check, he wondered if perhaps Penny had broken character and snapped. It wouldn't be the first time something like that happened. Not having her available to answer his questions was frustrating him. Seth wanted to believe in her innocence, but he had to admit to himself, if not to Gillian, that the news the sheriff had brought was unwelcome. At the very least, it wouldn't make Allison Cole's job defending her any easier.

"Gillian, why don't you try your cell phone again? I'd like to talk to Ace a second."

She walked over to the diner's pay phone, then after putting a few coins in and dialing the number, she handed the receiver to Seth.

Ace answered, "Hello? Gillian?"

"No, it's Seth. Any luck?"

"I'm about ready to give up, I can't find her anywhere downtown. I'm not ready to throw in the towel yet, though. I don't think she'd go anywhere near the water, but I'm going to check a few shanties this afternoon."

"Ace, did you know Penny spent some time at Brolin?"

After a hesitant pause, he said, "So? A lot of my friends have, what's the big deal?"

"The big deal is that most of your friends aren't being accused of murder. You should have told us, Ace."

"I didn't want you to think Penny killed that woman

because she was crazy." Weakly, he added, "I wasn't sure you'd want to help if you knew."

"Well, we know now. What was she in for?"

"I never got the full details, but she's well now, I'm telling you there's no way she killed Vera Hobart."

Seth frowned into the telephone. "Anything else you're holding back you might want to share with us?"

There was a distinct pause, then Ace said, "No, not anything that has to do with Penny. Listen, I've got to go now."

After they were disconnected, Gillian said, "What's wrong? I've seen that look on your face before."

"Ace is lying to us, but I can't figure out why. He admitted to knowing about Penny's stays at Brolin, but when I asked him if there was anything else he wanted to share, I got the distinct impression he was holding something else back."

"That's just the cop in you."

Seth shook his head. "Maybe so, but the next time we see Ace, I'm not going to let him out of my sight until I find out what's really going on with him."

Vera Hobart must have touched a great many lives in Jackson's Ferry. There wasn't a place to park within a quarter of a mile of the Shrewsberry Mortuary where the funeral was being held. Seth had offered to let Gillian off at the door, but she'd refused. As he finally found a spot, the gravid dark sky finally started to seep above them, a fine mist turning into a steady rain.

As Seth retrieved his umbrella from behind the truck's front seat, he said, "Are you regretting you didn't take me up on my offer for curb service to the door?"

"It could be a hurricane and I wouldn't have. I should tell you, I'm not really fond of funerals."

"Who is? I think they're pretty morbid myself." He glanced at her huddled close to him. "I've got to admit, though, you look pretty stunning in black."

"I'm serious, Seth."

"I am, too. I was just trying to lighten your mood. Maybe this would be a good time to talk about something that's been on my mind."

Gillian smiled. "Anything to change the subject."

"Sorry, this is right along those lines." As they walked, he held the umbrella's protective shell closer to her. The rain was definitely picking up. He continued. "After Melissa's funeral, I decided I wasn't going to put anybody I loved through that kind of circus. My lawyer has orders in my will to have me cremated as soon as legally possible, along with strict instructions that there'll be no memorial of any kind." He stopped walking and looked directly into her eyes. "You don't have to do this if you don't want to, I'll understand, but I was kind of hoping you'd scatter my ashes over the tree farm after I'm gone."

Gillian was silent so long, he broke in, "I'm sorry, it was a bad idea. I just--."

She interrupted, and with a catch in her voice, she said, "I'd be honored. I've always planned on being cremated myself, I just never could decide where. Would it be asking too much if you'd do the same for me? Your farm is one of my favorite places on earth."

Seth whooped in delight. "Are you kidding? That sounds great. Just think of all the trouble we can get into throughout eternity. We'll have a blast."

Gillian grinned slightly. "You're a nut, you know that?" As she offered him a kiss, she added, "But you're my kind of nut. Don't ever change."

There was a huge canopy in front of the mortuary, and Seth shook the water from his umbrella, then leaned it against a stack of others belonging to the mourners already inside. Gillian touched his arm. "Do we have to go in just now?"

"No, we can wait a minute or two. Are you going to be all right?"

She nodded. "Just give me a chance to compose myself."

As they stood together, Lex Bascum hopped out of a cab and rushed to join them. "Am I late?"

Seth shook his head. "No. What happened?" Though she'd tried to cover it with makeup, he could see angry welts on her face, as if she'd been clawed.

Lex touched her cheek lightly. "I had to take Princess in for her shots this morning. She was fine until we got her onto the table, and then she turned into a one-cat demolition crew. I'm seriously considering letting my husband have her in the divorce settlement." She lowered her voice, though no one else was outside with them. "Have you two heard anything?"

Gillian said, "No, how about you?"

Lex's eyes seemed to gleam. "Last night at The Oak, Councilman Garska got a snootfull and declared his undying love for Vera to the world. Can you believe it?"

Seth said, "We were there. It wasn't anything like that, Lex. He was just mourning a friend's loss."

"So you're an expert on Vera's life now, are you? I suppose all those midday visits the councilman paid on Vera were platonic, too." Quickly, she added, "Vera was right next door, I couldn't have missed it if I'd wanted to. Poor thing, I don't think she was ever truly happy with her lot in life." Lex looked out into the rain. "Then again, are any of us? Well, I'd better get inside. You two coming?"

"In a minute."

Lex shrugged, then hurried inside.

Seth said, "News certainly travels fast in Jackson's Ferry, doesn't it?"

"Remind me never to do anything I'd be ashamed of."

Seth put an arm around her. "Now what fun would that be? At the very most I'll agree to shutting the curtains first."

She nudged him gently. "I'm okay now. We might as well go on in."

Chapter 12

Gillian hadn't wanted to say anything to Seth, but she dreaded going to funerals in the same way embezzlers felt about being audited. Her aunt Sarah had died when Gillian was a little girl, and her parents had forced her to go the funeral, a full affair of mourning held deep in the Carolina mountains Sarah had called home. There'd been so much open weeping and gnashing of teeth, Gillian had been afraid the mourners were possessed, whether by demons or angels she couldn't say. Surprisingly, the woman in the open casket didn't look like Aunt Sarah at all. Too much makeup, a hairdo she'd never have allowed in life, and a stiff horizontal form all betrayed the spirit of the woman when she'd been alive. Sarah had been in constant motion her entire life, and Gillian had always secretly suspected her of sleeping while she was standing up. Gillian had agreed to her father's funeral more for the people mourning him than any sense of closure she needed for herself. She had nursed him through the final stages of the cancer that had whittled away at him until there was nothing of the man she loved left inside the fragile shell.

At least at Vera's funeral she had no tangible personal ties with the deceased.

There were flowers everywhere, spilling from the front altar down both sides and nearly filling the back of the room as well, their mingling scents were almost overwhelming. Gillian could see cards from the Junior League, the Jackson's Ferry country club and even from the charity board Gillian traded for. Vera had been a joiner, and now it showed. She wished all the money spent for blossoms that would quickly fade had been put where it could do some good, to the charities Vera had supported in her life. Gillian felt herself grow angry, wondering how many blankets the total would buy for the shelter, how many meals could be served to the starving. All she could think of was what a waste it all was. She gazed for a moment at the open casket from twenty feet away. Was this what Vera had wanted, to be displayed among a floral showcase?

"Are you all right?" Seth whispered to her.

"I'm fine. It's just a little too much."

Seth's eyebrows rose. "Think how much good the money spent on these flowers could have done. What a waste."

She patted his cheek softly. "You always know the right thing to say."

"You usually get upset when I'm crabby," he said with a smile.

"Only when it's not justified. I couldn't agree with you more about all of this."

"So let me get this straight. If I agree with you, my complaints are justified. Otherwise I'm just a crabby old man, is that it?"

"I wouldn't say you're that old, would you?"

"Let's just mingle a little and see what we can hear, okay?"

Gillian nodded. "That's fine. Don't go too far, though. It's nice having you close by."

He touched her shoulder lightly. "I feel the exact same way about you."

Gillian watched Seth drift away, but she stood watching the crowd of people a few moments before she could bring herself to join any particular group of mourners. The room was full of people in every shade and style of black imaginable. Bradley Hobart was holding court in front of the room, looking a little too much in grieving to match the man she'd spoken to before. She saw Sandi, away from the main group, staring daggers toward the front of the room, whether at Vera's shell or Bradley himself Gillian couldn't say. Was there trouble in paradise?

Jason was scowling to one side off by himself, and it looked as if no one dared approach him. Lex was talking with a group of women all dressed in designer outfits. It was the country club crowd, a clique Gillian had no interest at all in joining. In the very back of the room, she saw Seth talking in hushed tones with Sheriff Kline, still dressed in his police uniform. She wondered what they were discussing, but from the looks on their faces, she wasn't sure she wanted to butt in.

Kevin Garska was sitting alone in a chair near the front, his gaze riveted to Vera's body. Gillian was about to offer him her condolences when a man's voice behind her said, "You look as lost as I feel. I never know what to do at these things."

Gillian turned to find Lex's husband Travis there. They didn't know each other all that well, but sometimes at funerals it was important for people to find someone they could talk to. Gillian always suspected it was a way to keep the reality of their own mortality at arm's length.

"There certainly are a lot of flowers, aren't there," she said, offering small talk.

Travis said, "Oh, yes, Vera had a lot of friends." The sarcasm in his voice startled Gillian, and she could smell liquor on his breath.

"You two didn't get along that well?"

Travis waved a hand in the air. "This isn't the time or the place to go into it. I'm here to pay my respects and get out without fighting with Lex."

"I'm sorry about your breakup. Lex told me earlier."

"I bet she didn't tell you why, did she?"

Now what in the world could she say to that? "She said there were some problems, that's about all."

"What could she have said, that she was sleeping around and I caught her? That good old Vera up there was the one who told me what was going on? I doubt she told you anything that even remotely resembled reality. My soon-to-be ex-wife has trouble with the truth sometimes." He drew closer to her and said, "Let me give you a hint. You can tell she's lying whenever you see her lips move."

"She told me you ran off with your secretary."

"Yeah, well, she told me she was always faithful, too, and that wasn't true either." He looked around the room in disgust, then said, "Now if you'll excuse me, I'm getting out of here. I've made my appearance, and suddenly I can't stand being in the same room with her." As he nodded toward Vera's coffin, he added, "It's an honest shame she couldn't have been the star of this show herself." His glance went to Lex, who was watching the conversation out of the corner of her eye.

As Travis walked off, Gillian saw Lex excuse herself from her group and headed straight for her. In clipped words, she said, "I can't believe he had the gall to show his face here. What did he say about me?"

Gillian didn't like Lex's accusatory tone, but she held her own temper. "We were just discussing Vera."

"I'll bet. Did he tell you I was sleeping around, too? He'd do anything to justify his behavior."

Gillian pushed a little. "He said Vera told him you were having an affair."

"For God's sake, why would he say something like that? He must be drunk."

Gillian admitted, "I thought I smelled alcohol on his breath."

"There, I told you. Dutch courage is the only courage Travis ever had. Let me set this straight, I wasn't having an affair with anybody." In disgust, she added, "With my track record with men, I think I'm going to give them up entirely. They're not worth the trouble."

"I wouldn't say that about all of them."

Lex said, "Yeah, well you must have one of the few good ones left. Me, I think I'm done with the whole lot of them." Suddenly changing her tone, Lex glanced up at the casket as she said, "Didn't they do a wonderful job with Vera? She looks so natural. And she would have loved these flowers. I think Jackson's Ferry really did right by her."

Natural? Gillian thought Vera's face looked like a waxed image of itself. As for the flowers, she suddenly realized that

Lex was probably right. Vera probably would have loved them. She would have equated the dollars spent on floral arrangements with the degree she'd been loved by everyone, though that was obviously not the case.

Seth joined the two of them as people started taking their seats. Lex said a hurried, "Good to see you again," then headed back to her group.

Seth and Gillian moved to the back of the chapel and took the two seats nearest the door. Once they were seated, Seth said, "What was that all about? I saw you talking to Travis, and the next minute Lex was over there grilling you."

"Travis said Lex was the one sleeping around, and that Vera was the one who told him. I wouldn't put much stock in it, though, he's been drinking. What was so important you and the sheriff were discussing?"

"He thinks the murderer's going to show up at the funeral, so he's ready to grab Penny if she walks in the door."

"Penny would have to be crazy to show her face around here." After she'd said it, she realized it had been a poor choice of words, considering the woman had been institutionalized at one point in her life. "You know what I'm saying."

"I know exactly, and I agree with you." She watched Seth as he hesitated, then said, "Listen, any reason we need to stay for the eulogy? I figure we can catch up with everybody at the gravesite ceremony, and neither one of us wants to sit through the service." It was obvious the prospect of enduring the funeral made him as uncomfortable as it did her.

"Let's go before anyone notices."

As they sneaked through the door, Gillian heard the organ music that had been playing softly in the background start to swell.

They'd made their escape just in time.

Outside, the rain had stepped back to a drizzle, and Gillian could see a gap in the cloud cover. "I think it's going to stop raining soon."

"Is that part of your ancestry telling you?" He often teased her about her United Nations gene pool, while she countered with jibes about his own white-bread heritage.

"No, I heard a weather report earlier and they said the rain would end before sunset. What should we do before we go to the cemetery?"

"Tell you what, why don't we skip the graveside service altogether and go out to the farm. There's nothing we can do for a while here, and I kind of miss my place."

Gillian smiled softly. "Okay, I get the hint. I still think we should stay together while we're in the thick of this investigation. How about if tonight we stay at your place?"

Seth kissed her lightly. "Tell you what, just for that, I'll fix you a meal after the wake that'll top any chef in town."

"It's a date."

Back at the cottage, Gillian chided, "Seth, don't you ever check your messages? You've got three of them on your answering machine."

Seth said, "There's nobody I need to talk to who's not already here. We just saw Grady, he's fine, and I'm with you. Anybody else can wait until I get around to getting back to them."

"You've got a real cavalier attitude. I hate not knowing if somebody's trying to reach me."

Seth wrapped her into his arms. She felt strong on her own, an independent woman who could make her own choices in life and stand fast by herself. Then why did it feel so good in his embrace? She didn't question it, she just enjoyed it. After all, wasn't that what it meant to be a modern woman, to be able to choose the role she wished to play in life?

"Your business is a little different from mine. Nobody's going to call me with an emergency Christmas tree order, not in May, anyway." He released her, then hit the replay key on the machine. As it rewound, he said, "Feel better?"

"Much."

The first message was from an old friend in Charlotte just wanting to catch up.

They never did hear what the last message was.

The second voice that came over the speaker was obviously distorted by some sort of machine. The sex of the caller was unrecognizable, but the intent of the message was not.

"Those shots an hour ago were a warning. It's the last one you'll get. If you haven't butted out of Vera Hobart's death by tomorrow noon, something drastic's going to happen. Don't think you're safe just because you were a cop. I could have dropped your girlfriend just as easily as you."

Seth hit the rewind button and listened to the message a few more times, impatient as the initial message always replayed first in the queue. Finally, Gillian said, "It's a little too late for that particular warning to do any good, isn't it?"

"I wouldn't let it worry you. This just means we're managing to ruffle some feathers. I doubt Penny would have the money for a voice scrambler, those gizmos aren't cheap. It just makes me believe that much more that she's not involved in the murder."

"She's involved all right. Somebody's trying to frame her, and they don't like us snooping around."

"Well, they're going to have to just live with it." He rubbed her shoulder gently. "I'm glad you're staying close while we're looking into this."

Gillian said, "Are you under the impression I can't take care of myself?"

"Are you kidding? I was kind of hoping you'd be able to protect me if things got rough."

Like always, he managed to defuse the tension by lightening the mood. Still, there was a new, darker undertone to their time together as they awaited the wake service. They managed to occupy their time with a few glasses of wine and a couple of games of chess, but Gillian couldn't keep her mind on the outcomes and Seth won easily, though they usually battled even in their matches.

He picked up on her mood and said, "That's enough chess, don't you think?" Seth looked at a Shaker clock on the wall, a piece he'd built himself. "It's close to time for the wake anyway. Why don't we be the first ones there so we can find out what happened in case we missed anything."

"Like a graveside confession? Do you think Hobart's going to be that easy to nail?"

Seth raised one eyebrow. "Since when did you narrow in on him? We've still got Jason, Kevin Garska, Sandi and who knows who else. I for one am not ready to give up on the rest of them and focus on Hobart."

"Seth, are you telling me you honestly believe Councilman Garska could have killed her? Did you see him at the funeral? He couldn't take his eyes off Vera's body. It was true love, there's no doubt in my mind."

"It could have been true guilt. He wouldn't be the first murderer who felt remorse and grieved at his victim's funeral. If he was over there as much as Lex said he was, maybe there was more going on between the two of them than he was willing to admit."

Gillian pursed her lips. "So he dressed up as homeless lady and stabbed Vera over a lover's quarrel? It doesn't exactly qualify as the heat of the moment, does it?"

"I've seen stranger things happen, but I'm not so sure we can take the eyewitness's word on what happened."

"He's a priest, for God's sake, Seth. When did you suddenly become so distrustful?"

"Since you dragged me into this investigation." He held his hands up, staving off her protest. "Okay, I admit I'm doing this willingly. I feel like a little part of me was lost and it's back in place now. Even if the eyewitness is telling exactly what he saw, which I'm only conceding for the sake of argument right now, you've got a point. It could have been anybody dressed as a homeless person, man or woman, who stabbed Vera. We know one thing for sure, it had to be premeditated, or else why wear a disguise."

Gently, Gillian asked, "Why the sudden bad mood? Is something bothering you?"

After a few seconds of silence, he said, "I'm sorry, Gillian, funerals have that affect on me. It is true, though, I wish I knew how we managed to put such a scare into the killer. I don't feel like we've accomplished much at all so far."

"You know the drill, Seth, Dad certainly pounded it into me. You keep gathering information until you have enough to get at the truth. I've got a feeling once the liquor starts flowing this evening at the wake we're going to hear more than we hoped for."

He kissed her tenderly, then said, "Thanks for putting up with me."

With a grin, she said, "It's a real burden sometimes, but all in all I think you're worth the trouble."

Seth's black mood was lifted. "Thanks for the vote of confidence." He clapped his hands together and rubbed them fiercely. "So let's go to this wake and see if we can trip anybody up. I wouldn't mind getting another drink or two into Kevin Garska. I've got a suspicion he's still holding something back."

As Gillian put on her coat, she said, "Do you think he's crazy enough to drink again after his performance last night?"

"If he doesn't on his own, maybe we can give him a little prodding."

"You're a wicked, wicked man, do you know that?"

"Don't think you're the first one to tell me that. Now let's go before we miss something."

By the time they arrived at The Clusters restaurant the first mourners were already there. The Clusters had been around forever, one of those restaurants that seemed to change its menu or its owners every few years, yet still somehow managed to stay in business.

The walls of the dining room were done in dark heavy paneling, with brass sconces shedding sparse light into the central room. They'd obviously been turned up to their full strength for the wake, but Gillian still found it too dark for her tastes. That's why she loved her loft so much, there was always open space and plenty of light. The Oak was the same way, now that she thought about it.

She had to admit, though, that part of The Clusters versatility was that the main dining area could be closed off in sections, thus easily allowing for private parties of just about any size. Where The Oak was basically just one large room, The Clusters also offered a grouping of private dining rooms in the rear that connected through a maze of doors that could be closed or opened to accommodate several groups at once. For Vera's wake, Hobart had gone all out, renting a good three-quarters of the entire place, including the bar, the main dining area, and a few of the rooms in back. A buffet table loaded with food was located in the largest open space, with tables set up in long rows to allow the mourners to sit together while they ate. Gillian doubted anybody would choose the smaller, more intimate spaces considering the circumstances. At funerals and wakes, it had been her experience that people generally hated to be alone.

Hobart was near the front door greeting people as they came in, and Gillian could see his back stiffen when she and Seth walked inside.

He managed to say politely, "Good of you to come," though there was no sincerity in his voice.

Seth matched his tone exactly as he replied, "So sorry for your loss," before they stepped past him.

Out of his hearing, Gillian said, "I don't think he likes us. That wasn't exactly a heartfelt exchange of mourning."

Seth shrugged. "I don't know about you, but I'm not going to lose any sleep over it tonight. Should we break up and mingle or stick together?"

"I think we'd better separate. We can learn more that way, then we can compare notes later."

Seth nodded. "Okay, just don't load up on the buffet, I'm still planning to cook for you tonight after we're through here."

He went straight to a group of older men in one corner, and Gillian recognized several of them as members in good standing of the TriCorners Club, a gaggle of men who met every morning for breakfast at the TriCorners Dairy Center counter to talk about everything from the weather to whoever was currently screwing up the country to the length of women's skirts. She knew Grady was a member in good standing whenever he came into town for breakfast, and Seth had shared a few hilarious accounts with her on those rare days he was invited to sit in. It wasn't a club you could petition to join, new memberships were offered on invitation only, and there were several civic leaders who belonged to a dozen organizations who would have loved to be invited, if only for a single breakfast. Nobody could figure out a rhyme or reason as to why certain people were invited to sit in or to join, or more likely, to be ignored completely. One thing was certain, money or political power didn't count; the mayor was shunned, while two of the five town councilmen and the city planner were all members. The president of Jackson's Ferry Bank and Trust belonged, but then so did Grady, a man who'd never been financially successful in any of his careers, though he'd led a long and interesting life.

Gillian wasn't surprised they liked Seth, he had a quality about him that people responded to. With unerring accuracy, she realized he'd just tapped into an excellent source of information. If anything was going on, in front of or behind the scenes in the entire county, the TriCorners Club would know about it.

Gillian realized she'd better get busy if she was going to garner any information of her own to share.

She hadn't meant to start with Sandi Ingalls, but they made eye contact and Sandi looked as if she needed someone, anyone she could grab, to talk to.

Sandi walked rapidly over to Gillian and said, "Now I

know how a leper feels." She lowered her voice, "Does everyone in the room know about Bradley and me?"

"We're in a small town, Sandi. It doesn't take long for word to get around." Gillian looked closer at the girl's reddened eyes. "Have you been crying? Don't tell me you've been mourning the death of your competition."

"It's not that, it's just that Bradley's being so mean about everything. He won't have anything to do with me, and he even yelled at me."

This could be good. Gillian said, "Tell me what happened," trying to look as sympathetic as she could.

It was all the prodding Sandi needed. "He stayed behind after the graveside ceremony, so I thought he wanted to talk. I waited until everyone else was gone, then walked up and put my arm around him." With a hint of defiance in her voice, she said, "It wasn't in a sexual way, I was just trying to give him my support. He jerked away from me like my touch was poison, then he snapped at me. He said, 'I need some time alone, for God's sake. Don't you have any decency in that little black heart of yours?' Well, I wasn't about to take that, not after what I'd been through. 'You wanted her dead just as much as I did, so don't try to deny it.' He looked really shocked. 'I was married to her for sixteen years, I wanted a divorce, I didn't want to see her dead.' He pushed me away, and I almost fell onto the grave, what with the rain and the soft soil from their digging. I almost didn't come over here, but I'm not letting him get by with throwing me away like some kind of trash. He told me he was going to marry me if he ever got free, and by God, he's free now, isn't he?"

Hobart had been watching the conversation. He came towards Gillian and Sandi with fire in his eyes. "Can you keep your mouth shut? There's no reason you have to tell the world what's on that little tiny mind of yours."

Raising her voice so everyone could hear, Sandi said, "Are you trying to get rid of me?"

Hobart said, "You're not welcome here, you weren't

invited, and you certainly weren't any friend of my wife's."

"No, but I was sure a friend of yours."

His words now low with rage, Hobart replied, "Get out of here, before I throw your skinny little tail out the door myself."

The force of the verbal blow weakened her. Gillian took Sandi's arm gently. "Come on, I'll walk you out."

Sandi nodded numbly as Gillian led her outside. Most of the people in the room had been following the exchange with great interest, but as the two of them walked out of the Clusters, everyone's eyes went purposely to the floor or to the walls, anything to avoid personal contact with the scorned woman.

Ironically, a beam of sunlight broke through the breaking clouds as they walked outside. Gillian looked at Sandi and saw that she was still stunned over her treatment. She asked softly, "Are you going to be all right?"

"Don't worry about me, I'm going to be fine." With a stronger, harsher tone to her voice, she said, "He's sadly mistaken if he thinks he can get rid of me that easily, not after what I did for him."

"What exactly did you do?"

Sandi's head spun around and looked at Gillian as if she hadn't realized for a moment she'd spoken aloud. "Never mind. Thanks for getting me out of there before I exploded. I've got to go, I've got something I need to take care of." Before Gillian could probe any deeper, Sandi was storming to the parking lot for her car.

When Gillian walked back inside the restaurant alone, several people nodded at her approvingly, and Hobart himself came over to her. "Thanks for getting her out of here. I'm sorry you had to hear that. Sandi's got a really active imagination. She took a few harmless flirtings and built them into something much bigger than they were."

Gillian said coolly, "She didn't sound like she was fantasizing to me."

Hobart iced her with a glare, then said, "Whatever. Like

I said, thanks for handling it."

As he walked away, Gillian wondered about the cause of the scene. Hobart had acknowledged he'd been after Vera for a divorce, but she had to admit, with his wandering eye it wasn't likely he was going to tie himself down with another wife, at least not anytime soon. While she didn't doubt he'd had an affair with Sandi, it was also obvious to everyone in the room that now that Bradley Hobart was free, he was done with the young sales clerk. What had Sandi meant about 'all that she'd done for him'? Was it an unconscious admission of guilt? She needed to find Seth and tell him exactly what Sandi had said.

As Gillian looked around the room for him, she saw Jason Skyles watching her, a cryptic expression on his face. When he saw that she's noticed his attention, he joined her.

"So what did Hobie's little playmate have to say outside?"

"She was upset, there's no question about that."

From the glass of amber fluid in his hand and the exaggerated pronunciation in his words, Gillian knew that if Skyles wasn't drunk, he was well on his way. Seth had warned her that he was mean when he was drinking, so she knew she'd have to watch her step.

Surprisingly, the young man laughed. "I'll just bet she was. Good old Hobie couldn't wait to get rid of Vera so he could be with her, but I'm betting Sandi lost a lot of her appeal to him when he suddenly found himself free." He took a healthy drink, wiped his lips on the sleeve a jacket that ill fitted him, then said, "She was mine once, you know."

Gillian raised her eyebrows in inquiry, hoping he'd go on, and silently waited for him to go on.

Skyles readily filled the void. "I made the mistake of taking Sandi to dinner at Vera's, it was kind of a peace gesture, you know? The only problem was, Hobie found Sandi more fascinating than the dessert, and the next thing I know she's dumping me to be with him."

"That had to really hurt."

The young man's eyes narrowed, and Gillian saw a flash of overwhelming anger cross his face. It was gone as suddenly as it had came, but there was no mistaking the raw, feral power in his eyes. "The two of them deserve each other."

He finished his glass, put the empty down on the nearest table, then headed back for the bar without another word. As he walked away, Gillian felt a wash of relief flood through her. There was no denying the intensity of Jason Skyles' emotions. If Bradley Hobart had died instead of his wife, Gillian would have been willing to bet even money that the young man had done it. But kill his mother? She didn't think so. Unless somehow she'd tried to intercede on her husband's behalf and she'd gotten in the way. From the way he dressed and acted, Skyles could easily be mistaken for a denizen from the streets, but Gillian had a hard time believing he'd dress up as a woman, let alone premeditate anything. He appeared to be a man of action, not a careful planner. She watched him collect another drink, then stomp out the door, probably to drink alone. Gillian approached the bartender and said, "I think you'd better stop serving him alcohol. He's had enough."

The bartender looked surprised. "What, of club soda? There's just enough booze in those glasses to give them color, I doubt he can even taste it, let along feel anything. Strange, he looks like a real drinker, doesn't he?"

Gillian said, "Sorry to bother you," then left in search of Seth. She wanted to discuss with him why Jason would give the appearance of drinking when he was probably as sober as he'd been in days. Was he up to something, or was it that he couldn't trust his tongue when he was drunk? Maybe she'd been premature dismissing him as a suspect.

Regardless, she wanted a chance to speak with him again, to see if she could figure out his game. She went in search of her coat and was surprised to find Kevin Garska in the room where the coats were being temporarily stored, alone with a bottle of bourbon in his hands. He wasn't even bothering with a glass, though the seal on the lid was still unbroken. Gillian asked, "Are you all right?"

He waved the bottle in the air. "This? I haven't had a drop. I just want it here to keep me company."

He didn't sound drunk, and Gillian had seen enough of his performance the night before to know it was something he wouldn't be able to hide. "Why don't you give the bottle to me? I'll hold it for you, okay?"

Garska stared at the bottle a few moments, then handed it over to her. "Drinking's not going to solve anything, is it? I should have learned that last night. It's just all so final, you know what I mean?"

Gillian sat beside him on an empty chair. "I do, there's no explaining it. It's like a part of your life's gone forever, and you don't have the slightest bit of control over it."

Garska smiled through his pain. "That's it exactly. There was so much I wanted to tell her, so much we could have done together, only she wouldn't listen to me, she wouldn't do what I asked."

What did he mean by that? Gillian said, "You tried, though, didn't you? Were you angry with her?"

"Angry? I was furious. She knew what Hobart was up to, yet she wouldn't leave him. I'd just about lost my patience with her." He stared at his hands, then looked surprised when he realized that they were clinched into fists. As he opened them back up, he said softly, "We had a fight."

"What happened?" Was she getting an inadvertent confession? She had to keep him talking. "You can tell me."

They both saw the shadow in the doorway at the same time. Gillian wished whoever it was would go away, but Garska jumped to his feet and hurried to the doorway. "I should have known you'd be close by. Spying on me?"

Seth said calmly, "I was looking for Gillian."

Garska looked at him a second, then snapped, "Well you found her." He reached down and pulled the bottle from Gillian's hands. "I don't know why I thought I could trust you, you're just like all the rest."

After he was gone, Seth said, "I'm sorry. I saw you disappear back here, and when you didn't come back out I started to worry about you. Did he tell you anything?"

"I think he was about to confess, if you want to know the truth." Gillian let her anger flow into her words, and the impact on Seth was immediate.

"Hey, I said I was sorry. You really think he killed Vera to keep her from being with anyone else?"

"I didn't before, but I swear he sounded more remorseful than grieving to me just now." As quickly as it came, her anger was gone again. "So what did you find out?"

Seth smiled. "Too much to go into now. The party's breaking up, so why don't we go back to my place so I can fix you that meal I promised you?"

"It's a deal. I never knew asking questions could be so exhausting."

Seth took her in his arms. "That just means you're doing it properly."

As they collected their coats and said their good-byes, Gillian couldn't keep from wondering which one of the people she'd seen was capable of plunging a knife into Vera Hobart's chest.

Chapter 13

Thirty minutes after they got back to his place, Seth was preparing to stir fry some Chinese vegetables in his wok when the telephone rang.

He called out to Gillian, "Would you mind getting that? My hands are full."

Gillian laughed. "What if it's your other girlfriend?"

"I'll have to know which one it is before I can answer that question. It's probably just another wannabe. Take her name and number and I'll try to make room for her somewhere in my schedule."

As she reached for the phone, Gillian said, "Seth Jackson, humanitarian to the lonely women of Tacawba County." The smile quickly disappeared as she uttered a few words into the receiver, then added a quick, "We'll be right there," then she hung up the telephone.

Seth asked, "Who was it?"

Gillian was smiling widely. "It was Ace. He just saw Penny downtown."

As they drove into town toward the block Ace had given Gillian as his location, Seth said, "Tell me everything he said again."

"He was hunting for Penny when he saw her duck around a corner. Ace called her name but she must not have heard him. He ran after her, but by the time he got to the corner she was gone. He said he was going to keep looking for her, and that they wouldn't get far."

Seth said, "This is one of the few times in my life I wish I had a car phone."

"Do you think Allison Cole would be able to run right over here at the drop of a hat?"

Seth shook his head. "I'm afraid Allison's not in the picture any more, at least not until we get Penny safely in jail. Besides, I gave Harley Kline my word I'd call him the second I found Penny, and the sheriff's the kind of man who doesn't like to be lied to."

"You haven't seen her yourself, so technically you're not lying. Don't worry, we'll find a phone and call him as soon as we have Penny."

Seth grumbled, "Just like we should have done before. I knew the right thing to do, but I let myself be talked out of it. It was a mistake."

"Don't beat yourself up about it, there was no harm done. Penny's okay, we just have to help Ace track her down."

Seth was quiet the rest of the time it took to drive to Ace's location. As wonderful a woman as she was, sometimes Gillian just didn't understand. Whenever Seth ignored his gut reaction to something, he nearly always ended up regretting it. It had made him a good cop, but he was beginning to wonder if the years away from the job had taken the edge off his skills. One thing was certain; no one was going to talk him out of turning Penny into the sheriff, even if he had to kidnap the woman himself to do it. With her loose on the streets, she was in constant danger. Only when Penny was safely behind bars would Seth stop worrying about her. Maybe then he could spend more of his energy focusing on the real killer.

Ace was gone by the time they got to the location he'd given them, but Seth hadn't expected him to stand still. He whipped the truck into a parking space, there wasn't much of a demand for the spots in that section of town day or night, and they were both out barely after the truck came to a stop.

The second he was on the street, he started calling for Ace.

Gillian said, "How are we going to find him?"

"Did he say which direction he was going when he broke the connection?"

Gillian thought a moment, then said, "There, he went that way. He said he saw a barber pole as he turned the corner, and there used to be a barbershop over there. I used to go with Dad sometimes when he got his haircut."

As they hurried to the corner, he asked, "He came all the way over here for a trim?"

"Seth, Dad had a flattop, I could have cut it myself when I was twelve, but he liked to keep in touch with people; he used to say you never knew when you'd learn something. I can remember one day he had his hair cut three times. I think the barbers knew it too, it was like a game they played."

There were a few homeless people on the streets, a lone one here and there and a few in tight groups, but a quick glance showed that none of them were Penny or Ace.

They found him down the block clutching Penny's distinctive coat. At one time, it had been a fashionable leather knee-length jacket, sporting patches of different tints and shades of dyed material. But the jacket hadn't worn well over time, and many of the original colors had faded into varying shades of gray. There wasn't another coat like it in the world.

Seth said, "Where is she? Did you lose her again?"

Ace looked humiliated. "I turned the corner and she was gone. It was like she disappeared or something." He held the jacket up. "All I found was her coat."

"So why would she drop her coat, and more importantly, where did she go?"

"Seth, she loved this coat," Ace said. "It was her most valued possession in the world. There's no way I'm going to believe she just dumped it on the street."

Gillian said, "It doesn't matter why she did anything right now. All that matters is that she couldn't have gone far. Let's split up and see if we can find her."

Seth started to protest when Gillian took off down the street. He knew she could handle herself in just about any situation, but he still felt responsible for her. The streets could get ugly. He purposely chose a search path near hers, keeping one eye on Gillian as he called Penny's name.

Suddenly, Ace yelled, "Over here. Hurry."

Seth recognized the pain and anguish in Ace's voice, he'd

heard it too many times as a cop; he knew that whatever the man had found wasn't good.

It was even worse than he could have imagined.

Penny was swinging in the gentle breeze, hanging by the neck from a stout security light tethered by one of her own ragged scarves. Ace was scrambling to pull the body down as Seth approached. He brushed against her foot, and the body did a macabre dance in the air. Seth climbed on the pallet stack with Ace and said, "Get out of the way."

Ace moved numbly back to the ground as Seth checked Penny's throat for a pulse. Nothing. With gentle probing, almost as if he was afraid he'd hurt her, he probed her neck lightly. It was cleanly broken. She'd probably been dead the second her body felt the jerk of the homemade noose.

As he climbed down, Gillian came into the alley. She raised an eyebrow, and Seth shook his head. Ace said frantically, "What are you doing? You can't just leave her up there."

"There's nothing we can do now, Ace. She's gone."

Ace kept repeating almost as a mantra, "She deserves a chance, Seth, she deserves a chance."

"I said it's no use." Seth tried to think of something comforting to say to Ace, but he knew from experience how futile words were in times of great grief.

"At least cut her down," Ace whimpered. "Nobody else has to see her like this."

"I'm sorry, but we'd better leave things exactly like they are. The sheriff will want to see everything just the way we found it. Ace, can I have Gillian's phone? I need to call the police."

"Dammit, why would she kill herself? It doesn't make sense. Penny wouldn't do that."

Gillian stepped forward. "She was feeling trapped and frightened, Ace. Maybe she didn't think there was any other way out."

"She could count on me, she knew that."

Seth prodded harder. "The phone, Ace, give it to me."

Ace handed him the telephone and Seth dialed the number he knew by heart. After a short wait, he got Sheriff Kline on the line. "I found her, Harley."

"Son of a dog, it's about time she turned up. Now listen to me carefully, I don't want you to let her out of your sight, do you understand? If she gets away again, I'm holding you personally responsible, do you read me?"

"She's not going anywhere. She's dead."

After a pause and a push of breath, the sheriff said, "What happened?"

"It looks like she hanged herself."

"Tell me where you're at, I'll be right there."

Seth tried to distract Ace when the police cut Penny's body down after documenting the scene with photographs and videotape. The sheriff was going to make sure no one questioned his findings. Ace wouldn't look away though, insisting on watching every sway of the body. Two men waited below to catch the body as a third carefully severed the noose, but as Penny fell, the abruptness of the cut caught them off-guard and the body tumbled to the pavement. Seth had to hold Ace back from attacking the cops, and Gillian was finally able to calm him enough to get him away from the scene. Seth had worried about Gillian's first brush with a corpse dead through violent means, but she appeared to be holding up fine. He knew well enough that she still might be in shock, and that the visions might not come later until she dreamed. He'd experienced too many of those very same nightmares himself.

After Ace and Gillian were gone, Sheriff Kline said, "You know if you'd brought her to us when you found her the first time this never would have happened."

"Yeah, don't you think I've thought of that myself?"

"It's not like you to be sloppy, Seth, that's all I'm saying." After a moment of silence, he said, "At least it's all wrapped up for us. I'll say this for her, she saved the county the cost of a trial."

"I still don't think she killed Vera Hobart."

The sheriff frowned. "What, she killed herself because she lost her coat? Come on, it's pretty clear she was feeling remorse about what she'd done, so she ended it herself. Don't go stirring up trouble, Seth. I'm officially closing the case."

"She felt trapped, Harley. You told me yourself she'd been institutionalized. As long as things were going along on an even keel, Penny could manage. But having the whole county looking for her must have driven her over the edge. You can't close the case, there's too many things that aren't clear."

"Seth, do you have a single piece of hard evidence that supports what you're saying?"

Seth thought about all he and Gillian had learned. It was mostly gossip, rumor and innuendo, nothing he could take to the sheriff, let alone a grand jury. They weren't inclined to indict based on hunches.

The sheriff continued. "I didn't think so." He kicked at the ground, then said, "I'm not going to kid you, it's an election year and I don't mind having this thing wrapped up in one neat little package for me, but you know me better than to think I'd stop a murder investigation if I wasn't satisfied with the truth." He looked long and hard at Seth before he added, "Tell you what I'm going to do. You keep snooping around, as long as you're quiet about it, and if you find anything, you bring it to me and I'll think about reopening the case."

Seth started to say thanks when the sheriff held up his hand. "But I don't want one word getting back to me that you're saying Penny didn't kill Vera Hobart. You do, and I'm coming down hard on you, Seth, friend or no friend. Are we clear?"

Seth nodded. "Thanks for keeping an open mind."

"I'm not saying it's open, but I've had too many hunches myself that panned out, I'd be a damned fool to ignore yours, you were a good cop once." He grinned, then added, "And my Mama didn't raise any damned fools."

Seth walked out of the alley and found Ace and Gillian together on a nearby bench.

Gillian asked, "What did the sheriff say?"

"For now, the case is closed."

Ace said loudly, "Penny didn't kill Vera, and I know she didn't kill herself. She couldn't have."

"Take it easy, Ace. He gave us permission to keep looking around on our own, but I'm telling you now, Penny's death is going to make things that much harder on us."

Ace said, "I don't care. We've got to find the truth."

"We're not going to stop now, no matter what happens," Seth said reassuringly. "Penny's death is on the head of the murderer just as surely as if he'd put her neck in the noose himself."

Gillian said, "Why don't you come back with us tonight and sleep at Seth's place? You shouldn't be alone."

"Nobody's going to come after me now that Penny's dead."

"That's not why I made the offer," Gillian said. "I just don't think you should be by yourself."

Ace's eyes softened. "Thanks, but I kind of like it that way. I haven't slept under a real roof in so long I don't think I could breathe, let alone fall asleep. No, I'll be just fine." As he walked away, he said, "See you'all soon."

After he was gone, Gillian said, "What now?"

"There's nothing we can do tonight. Why don't we go back to my place and see if we can salvage dinner. Tomorrow, we'll start bright and early."

Gillian kissed him gently. "Thanks for sticking with this."

"You know me better than that, it's not exactly something I can give up on."

The next morning, Seth was finishing up breakfast while Gillian was enjoying a long hot shower. One of her only complaints about her loft was the lack of a reliable supply of hot water. When Seth had built his cottage, he had allowed himself the luxury of an oversized hot water heater, and Gillian loved to take advantage of it.

The phone rang, and he was surprised to hear Lex Bascom on the other end. "Did you hear the news? That crazy homeless woman who killed Vera hanged herself last night."

"Nobody knows for sure that Penny killed her, Lex."

"Come on, Seth, everybody in town's talking about the case being wrapped up. It's kind of an eloquent way to end things, isn't it?"

Seth snapped, "There's no end as far as I'm concerned. Gillian and I don't believe Penny killed Vera, we never did."

Lex said, "So that's why the two of you have been nosing around. Old Bradley was over here this morning complaining about you and Gillian playing Nick and Nora Charles, but I thought he was kidding."

"Is he the one who told you about Penny's death?"

"Yes, but that's not why he was over here. I think now that we're both single again he wants us to get together. In his dreams, maybe. What woman in her right mind would trust him after the way he cheated on Vera?" With an added twist of anger in her voice, she added, "I think he's got company, can you imagine the nerve? I can't believe you two are still going to investigate this when even the police think it's closed. If you ask me, you're both wasting your time." She laughed gently, then said, "But I guess it's your time to waste. I've got to go, somebody's at the front door. This place is getting busier than a lunch counter at high noon today. I can't wait to get out of town."

To be polite, Seth said, "Where are you going to move to? Have you decided yet?" As he spoke, Gillian came out of the shower wearing his white terry-cloth robe and rubbing her hair with one of his thick Egyptian Cotton towels. It was another little luxury he allowed himself. Looking at her wrapped up in it, he couldn't imagine a better way to spend his money. Gillian raised an eyebrow, and Seth held one finger up asking her to wait a moment.

Lex said, "No, all I'm sure about is that I'm going to get into my car and start driving until I get to a place where they don't know about grits or NASCAR or barbecue. This time tomorrow morning, I'll be on I-77 heading north."

"Well, if I don't see you again, good luck."

Lex almost cackled as she said, "I'm getting out of Hooterville, remember? You're the one who's going to be needing luck."

After they hung up, Gillian said, "Who was that?"

"Lex Bascom. She's heard about Penny's death last night, Hobart's already been over to her house."

"And she felt the need to give you an update?"

Seth frowned. "No, I think she wanted me to know she was leaving town. She's moving North."

Gillian looked appalled. "Now why would anybody want to leave lovely scenic Jackson's Ferry, North Carolina?"

Seth grinned. "I for one can't imagine. She also said she had the distinct impression Hobart was making a few moves on her as a going away present. Lex also said she thought he might have a houseguest, too."

Gillian said, "Now why am I not surprised by that?"

Seth asked, "Did you save me any hot water?"

Proudly, she responded, "Not a drop if I could help it. Don't worry, with that monster heater you've got, it's probably already built back up in the time it took you talk to Lex." Gillian finished hand-drying her hair, then wrapped it up in her towel like a modified turban. Seth saw the frown on her face and asked, "What's bothering you?"

"Lex calling here to update you on her moving plans. Do you think she was hoping for a shot at you herself before she left town?"

"Oh, yeah, I'm just a regular woman magnet."

"Seth, be serious. She might have wanted one last fling with a Southern Gentleman before she started going after the entire Yankee population of unattached men."

As he started to say something else, the telephone rang

again. Seth reached for it, but Gillian darted playfully in front of him and snatched it up. Before Seth could say a word, she added lightly as she covered the mouthpiece, "If it's Lex, I want to make sure she knows you didn't spend the night alone."

Gillian said confidently, "The Jackson residence."

The smile left her lips as she said, "Okay, I'll tell him," another pause, then she added, "we'll be right there."

Seth asked, "What was that all about?"

"I'm afraid you're going to have to skip that shower this morning. That was Sheriff Kline. You're not going to believe what he just found."

Chapter 14

"So don't keep me in suspense."
Gillian knew she should have let the sheriff speak with Seth when he'd called. It was just that she didn't want there to be any chance for Kline to refuse their visitation, so she'd ended the conversation as abruptly as she could. As she finished dressing, Gillian said, "Sheriff Kline wanted you to know that the case against Penny is wrapped up now. They found a note in her pocket asking for forgiveness."
"Wait a second, Ace told us Penny was illiterate. That proves the note's a fake. She didn't commit suicide, somebody just wanted us to think she did."
"That's why I told Kline we'd be right there. I hung up before he could tell us not to bother coming downtown. I for one want to see that note."
Seth agreed instantly.
In three minutes they were in the truck driving toward the police station. Seth said, "I still can't figure out why somebody would want Penny dead now. If they were going to kill her, they should have done it right after Vera's body was found. Where in the world has she been these last few days, anyway? This case is getting more confusing as we go along."
"It had to take somebody strong to force Penny up on those pallets. At least that should eliminate Sandi Ingalls from our list."
Seth shook his head. "Not if she used a gun to force Penny to do what she wanted. It still seems like a waste to kill her, not to mention the fact that it was as big a risk as killing Vera in the first place. No, Penny must have known something she didn't realize, and the killer couldn't afford to have her figure it out."
"Our pool of suspects were all at Vera's wake. The Clusters is close enough downtown so that it could place any

one of them at the scene."

Gillian thought about the people she'd seen there. Had any of them acted out of the ordinary? She had to admit that if she based her guesses on behavior, they'd all acted a little unusual during the wake. "We're going to have to ask each one of them where they were just after the wake. We couldn't trip anyone up with an alibi for Vera's murder, but this opens a whole new realm of possibility."

Seth smiled. "Good, that means we can drop the pretense that we're just concerned friends of Vera's and let everybody know we suspect them of murder. I'll take the chance of showing our hand over acting surreptitiously any day. Who knows? A little point-blank confrontation might just do the trick."

At the police station, Seth parked in the visitor's lot and they went inside. The sheriff was at his desk going through a stack of papers when Seth rapped sharply on his door frame. "Can we come in?"

With a grin, he said, "Seeing how you already are, it's a little late to ask, isn't it?"

"You're in a good mood, aren't you?"

The sheriff shrugged. "It's not exactly the textbook way to close a case, but it'll do." He looked at Gillian and said, "If you'd have given me a second, I could have told you to save yourself a trip. I'm not in any position to show you evidence in a case."

Gillian said, "That's why I didn't wait."

He shook his head. "It's not going to do you any good."

"Who's it going to hurt?" Seth said. "You said yourself the investigation's closed. There's something you should know, though. Penny was illiterate. That means she couldn't have possibly written that note."

"Come on, Seth, that one's a little weak, even for you. How did you happen to come across that information? It seems pretty convenient, especially if you want me to keep my investigation open."

"Would a witness to the fact help? I can produce him in

an hour if I need to."

The sheriff pushed a few papers around, then found the one he'd been looking for. "You mean this Ace character, I bet. He's not exactly the most credible witness I've ever heard of."

Gillian snapped, "Just because he's homeless doesn't mean he's a liar."

"Take it easy, I didn't say that. All I meant was that in this day and age it's hard to believe there's anybody in the county who still can't read or write."

"Then maybe you should come to the library on Tuesdays and Thursdays with me from four to five and tell that to the adults I'm teaching to read. We've got about a dozen people enrolled in our Adult Literacy program right now."

The sheriff at least had the decency to be caught off-guard by the news, but his reaction didn't surprise Gillian in the least. Adult literacy was one of the things that kept a lot of people from ever improving their position in life, but it was something nobody liked to talk about. Gillian always felt like it was magic when an adult read their first words. It was like having blinders suddenly removed and a new world opened up to them.

Seth said patiently, "Can we see the note, Harley?"

The sheriff studied him a few moments, then shrugged. "You're not likely to leave until I do, are you?"

"That's the joy of being semi-retired. I'm rarely in a great hurry to get anywhere."

The sheriff picked a photocopy off his desk and spun it toward Seth. "That's a copy, but I still want it back as soon as you look at it."

Gillian looked over Seth's shoulder and read, 'Can't go on. I'm so sorry,' scrawled in dark smudged letters on a scrap of a receipt for a candy bar from the Dollar Store dated three weeks earlier.

"Maybe your friend Ace was mistaken," the sheriff said. "It looks real enough to me. For all we know she got somebody else to write it for her before she killed herself.

No, I'm sorry, I'm not willing to open up this hornet's nest again based on an indigent's word."

Seth nodded grimly, then said, "Thanks for letting us see the note."

The sheriff shrugged. "Now if you two will excuse me, I've got a ton of other cases on my plate right now."

Outside, Gillian fumed, "He doesn't even want to believe us. What possible reason could Ace have for lying?"

"Take it easy. He's right about something. Unless we've got more solid proof that Penny was illiterate we're not going to convince anyone that that note is a fake." He kicked at a rock on the sidewalk, then said, "You know what? I'm glad we're out in the open. I'm tired of scurrying behind the scenes waiting for a crumb to drop. I'm ready to tackle some of our suspects head on with what we've learned."

"Do you have your gun with you? If you do, we can start right now."

Seth shook his head. "You know I don't normally carry it around with me."

"You don't normally confront possible double-murderers, either. I can't believe you wouldn't feel better if you had it with you."

Seth smiled, then pulled back his windbreaker. He was wearing his shoulder holster, the gun tucked in it.

Gillian said, "When did you put that on?"

"While you were in the shower."

"So you just walk right into the police station, armed, and nobody says a word to you? That doesn't do much for my faith in our law enforcement officers."

"It should. At least two cops saw I was carrying, not to mention Harley Kline. They all knew it before you did."

"You men all have suspicious minds, don't you?"

Seth laughed. "And women don't? Do we really want to have that particular discussion out here on the street?"

"No, I want to catch whoever's killing people and make them stop."

"Then let's get busy."

"Where do you want to start?"

"Let's go see the grieving widower. I'm dying to find out what he was up to last night right after the wake. If we're lucky, maybe his houseguest's still there."

It took a solid ten minutes of pounding on Bradley Hobart's door before he came out. Gillian had wanted Seth to give up. Several of the neighbors, including Lex Bascum next door, were peeking out behind drawn shades to see what the commotion was all about. Finally, Hobart opened the door wearing a bulky bathrobe and looking like he was sporting a major hangover. "Enough with the pounding. What in the world do you want this time of day?"

"It's not exactly the crack of dawn. Besides, I understand you've already had a chat with one of your neighbors, so it's going to be hard to sell that you just woke up. Do you have your clothes on under that robe?"

Hobart shook his head. "That blasted Lex couldn't keep her mouth shut with duct tape."

Seth continued, "We need to talk to you, and it can't wait. Can we come in?"

Instead of inviting them inside, Hobart narrowed the gap in the door. "Just tell me what you want."

"Okay, we can do this out here if you want to. Where were you last night from nine to ten PM?"

"Now why is that any business of yours?"

Gillian said, "We know you heard about Penny's hanging, but it wasn't a suicide."

"And you think I did it? I cared for my wife, but I'm not the type to go around seeking revenge on a homeless woman who killed her. It wouldn't bring Vera back."

Gillian said, "No, but it might have silenced a witness against you forever, especially if Penny saw you when you stole her knife."

"I didn't take her knife any more than I killed her last night."

Seth said, "And I suppose you can prove that?"

"Not to you, I won't. I heard you used to be a cop, but I don't see a badge now."

Seth crept closer to the doorway. "That's true, but I've got a lot of friends on the force. If you don't want to tell me, you can explain it all to them."

Hobart studied them a moment, then said, "Why not?" He turned back inside, and Gillian saw Seth's hand go to his shoulder holster as he moved his foot forward to block the door. Instinctively she took a step to the side to take herself out of the line of fire. Instead of any sudden moves though, Hobart yelled, "Come on out." When there was no response, he repeated, "Now!" with more force.

Sandi Ingalls came to the door, dressed in Vera's robe.

Gillian said, "I thought you two were fighting."

Sandi looked down at her feet. "We made up."

Seth asked, "Have you been here all night?"

Hobart said, "She was waiting out in my car after the wake. We had an argument, then we came back here. We've been together since seven last night."

"I wasn't asking you," Seth said.

Sandi nodded. "It's true."

Hobart snapped, "That's all they needed to hear. Now why don't you go get dressed?"

Sandi shot him a single dirty look before going upstairs. Seth said, "You've got a heck of a way to mourn, don't you?"

"Yeah, well that's none of your business either. I've answered your questions, now go away."

Seth pulled his foot back slightly as the door closed. Gillian said, "I can't believe that scum would sleep with his girlfriend the day he buried his wife."

"We knew Bradley Hobart wasn't going to win any Husband-of-the-Year contests. At least we know he and Sandi have alibis for last night."

Gillian snorted. "If they're telling the truth."

"You really think the two of them could agree on anything, let alone offer alibis for each other?"

"Maybe if they killed Vera together, thinking they'd get her insurance."

Seth shook his head. "Even if it were true, I can't see Hobart sharing the money with Sandi, let alone putting his head in her noose. I've got a feeling last night was just a fond farewell, whether Sandi knows it or not."

"So who does that leave?"

As they got into their truck, Seth said, "Greg Garska and Jason Skyles are at the top of my list now." He glanced at his watch. "Garska should be in his office all day, so we can be pretty sure he's not going anywhere. Why don't we head out to Jason's place and see what he's got to say for himself." As Seth drove, he said, "I think I'll let you ask him where he was last night. He seems to like you."

"What can I say, he's obviously a good judge of character." Before Seth could say anything, she added, "I know this is serious business, but you're right, I think Jason will tell me the truth."

"Don't give yourself too much credit. Besides, I'll be standing right there beside you."

"I wouldn't have it any other way."

As they started to drive away, Gillian looked back at the house Vera had lived in just a few days before. She might have been a gossip and a bit of a snob, but she didn't deserve a young chippie sleeping in her bed, wearing her bathrobe for God's sake, the day she was buried. At least Vera had tried to make the world a better place through her volunteer work. She wasn't perfect, but then who was? Words had never impressed Gillian all that much, it was action that counted, and whenever Vera had been called upon, she'd given freely of herself.

Gillian let her eyes drift to Lex's house and saw the curtains in the living room window suddenly flutter. Either the lady's forced air heat had just kicked on or she'd been watching the entire time. Gillian suddenly felt sorry for Lex, no matter what the cause of her life's downfall. She'd go through some tough times before she landed on her feet;

Gillian knew, she'd been there herself.

Sandi Ingalls and Bradley Hobart was a different matter entirely. She found herself hoping that Sandi found a way to trap Hobart into marriage. Gillian wouldn't put it past her, she'd managed to work herself back into Hobart's bed, and regardless of what Seth thought about farewell performances, from the look she'd just seen in Sandi's eyes, it didn't appear that the lady was going anywhere. The two deserved each other, and it would be a fitting punishment for the philandering widower.

As they drove up the long gravel drive to Jason Skyles' place, Seth said, "I don't see his truck, do you?"

"No. So if he's not home, why haven't you turned around yet?"

Seth smiled grimly. "Maybe he just wants us to think he's not there. His truck could be parked in back. One way or the other, I want to be sure."

Gillian knew that look in his eyes. He was up to something. "What are planning to do?"

In mock innocence, Seth said, "Me? I don't have the slightest idea what you're talking about."

They pulled up by the barn, and after a quick check of both places it was obvious Skyles was gone.

As Seth tested the door to the barn, Gillian said, "Are we ready to go?"

Seth held a finger to his lips as he looked at her. "Shhh. Did you hear that?"

Gillian hadn't heard a thing, other than a mockingbird going through its repertoire and a squirrel scolding it for being a noisy neighbor. "Nothing out of the ordinary."

"There it was again. It sounded like somebody inside might need our help."

It was obvious by the expression on her face that Gillian suddenly caught on. "Wait a second. Yes, I do believe I heard it that time. What should we do?"

Seth nodded his approval. "Why, we owe it to Mr.

Skyles to see if he needs our help." With a slight nod, he added, "I think we should try all the doors first, don't you? If we're wrong, we don't want him to know we've been here."

"Now what are the odds he just left a door or a window wide open for us?"

Seth shrugged. "It won't take long to find out, and I like it a lot better than breaking and entering."

"But you don't mind a little 'illegal entry' and 'trespassing', is that it?"

He ignored the jab. "Well, I guess we're going to have to do this the hard way." As he started to put his shoulder into the door, he paused and said, "I wonder," as he moved over to the big barn door. It didn't look like it had been moved in years, but Seth found the latch and miraculously the door easily swung open.

Gillian said, "I thought for sure he'd have boarded that thing up years ago."

"How else can he get some of those monsters he makes out of the barn? He doesn't want to be like the man who built a boat in his basement, then couldn't get it out."

Seth held the door open enough for her to get through, but Gillian hesitated. She was sure her father wouldn't have approved of the two of them breaking the law, no matter how justified they felt their reasons were. Sometimes Gillian could swear she felt her dad watching her from above, though she didn't agree with Seth's idea of Heaven and Hell at all. Seth was a die-hard Episcopalian, while her beliefs ran through a gamut of odd choices that ranged from her Indian heritage to Modern Individualism. Still, whenever Seth acted as a Lay Reader at church, Gillian was in the front pew offering her support. It wasn't hypocrisy on her part, she could see that there might have been a Creator of all things. She just didn't choose to worship Him the way most people did.

Seth interrupted her thoughts. "Come on, I don't want to be here when he gets back."

Gillian took a few steps forward and led the way inside.

The studio was well lit enough from its skylights for her to see where she was going. The sculpture Skyles had been working on before was off to one side, and Gillian saw a long graceful figure outlined by a handful of rods that somehow managed to capture motion.

Seth studied the piece a moment, then whistled softly. "He did it after all."

"What do you mean?"

"Don't you see it? He's sculpting you. I hate to admit it, but I think he's doing a good job of it, too."

"It could be anybody, Seth, I think you've got an overactive imagination."

Seth shrugged. "Whatever you say." As he started looking through the studio, Gillian said, "What exactly are we looking for?"

"Anything that might tie Jason to either murder."

"Well, as long as you're being specific."

"Gillian, I don't know. It could literally be anything."

She was looking through a row of heavy wooden boxes when she held something up for him to see. "Like maybe a worn, dirty dress big enough to fit him? Dressed in this, you'd look like you were a homeless woman yourself."

Seth took the garment in his hands. "Whew, it's got the right smell to it, doesn't it?" He dug into the pile, then said, "Too bad we can't find a wig, too." As he straightened up, he said, "Did you hear that?"

"I thought we were done with that game. We're already inside, aren't we?"

Then she heard it too. Outside, a car door slammed, and footsteps in the gravel were approaching the barn.

Chapter 15

Seth felt like a trapped rat. Even if he and Gillian could somehow manage to hide, his truck was outside in plain sight. From what he'd seen of Jason Skyles' temper, he'd better be ready for anything.

Gillian whispered fiercely, "What are we going to do?"

Instead of answering her, Seth called out loudly, "Skyles, where are you? Are you okay?" In a lower voice, he said, "I want him to think exactly what we said earlier. We heard noises and thought he might be in trouble."

"Do you really think he'll believe that?"

"I don't see too many other choices at the moment, do you?" Louder, he added, "Skyles, are you in here?"

The footsteps stopped at the barn door they'd left partially open, and Seth put a hand on Gillian's shoulder.

A woman Seth had never seen before walked through the door. She eyed Seth and Gillian suspiciously, then said warily, "What are you two doing in here?"

"We're looking for Jason Skyles, but he doesn't seem to be around."

With a snort of disgust, she said, "Why am I not surprised? He wasn't here last night, either. I swear, why does every artist with a shred of talent feel it gives them the right to eccentricity. I don't care, if he stands me up again, I'm going to demand he give me my deposit back and he can keep the mask." The woman walked to a nearby wall and touched a metal mask lovingly. It was cold and dark, but there was a humanity, a suffering in its features that drew the eye like a traffic accident, too morbid to look away. With near whispered breath, she said, "It truly is something, isn't it," as she caressed the cheekbones and strong jawline of the piece. "I have half a mind to leave the money on the bench and take this with me right now."

Seth asked, "You said he stood you up last night. Do you

happen to know what time that was?"

"Take your pick. I was here waiting in that awful car from six to ten, and he never showed up."

Gillian said, "His mother was buried yesterday afternoon. Did you know?"

The woman's features melted into softness. "No wonder he wasn't here. I drove up from Charlotte, I'm not from around the foothills. I had no way of knowing. I feel badly now, all the things I thought about him. The poor boy must be really suffering." Almost to herself, she added, "I wonder what he'll turn out next. Maybe I should wait on the mask." She touched it once more, as if it was a talisman. "No, I've got to have this, too." She looked pleadingly at Seth and Gillian. "If I give you the money will you pay him for me? I've got to get back to Charlotte tonight."

The last thing in the world Seth wanted to do was to admit to Jason Skyles that they'd been inside his studio without permission. He was about to decline when Gillian said, "Of course we will."

One look in Gillian's eyes told him it would be senseless to protest; she'd already made up her mind.

After the mask was carefully taken off the wall and loaded into the woman's front seat beside her, she waved as she drove away.

Seth said, "Now what do we do? Wait around for Skyles to come back and throw ourselves at his mercy? He could have us charged with trespass, you know."

Gillian smiled. "How could he do that, since he won't even know we're here?" She took a sheet of paper from her purse, jotted something on it, then folded it, along with the check, and laid it on the workbench. Seth asked, "What did you do, give him our phone numbers?"

"No, just a note of thanks from the new owner. This way everyone's happy. The lady has her mask and Skyles will have his payment."

Seth held the dress up. "And we've got the evidence. At least some of it." He looked at the soiled faded cotton in his hand. "I just wish Penny was still around to tell us if this dress belonged to the woman who shoved that ring in her hand."

"She's not, but didn't the sheriff say he had another witness? Let's go find that divinity student and see if he can help us."

Seth kissed her strongly, then said, "I'm glad at least one of us is thinking straight. I wasn't looking forward to asking Harley who the man was."

"You don't know his name do you?"

"No, but I can do one better than that. I can ask my parish priest."

One telephone call was all it took to get the seminarian's name and current address. Father Farabee, who'd known Seth since he'd moved to Jackson's Ferry, didn't even ask why he wanted the information. The two of them were close friends as well as priest and parishioner, and there was a bond of trust between them, as well as one of genuine friendship.

The address was in an austere apartment complex near the satellite seminary. Jackson's Ferry sported a minor though fine liberal arts college, a thriving community college and a small branch of the Episcopal seminary. It was one of the things that had attracted Seth to the community in the first place. He figured that a town with educational opportunities would provide a variety of traveling art exhibits and lecture series. Too, there would be a ready outlet for him if he ever decided to teach again. He felt at home in a college town, as if in some way he belonged.

A young man with clear gray eyes and an earnest expression met them at the door of the apartment.

Seth said, "Kyle Transom?"

"May I help you?"

"I'm a friend of Father Farabee's and I was wondering--."

The name brought immediate recognition, since Seth's priest taught a class or two at the seminary as an adjunct professor of advanced theological theory. "Please, won't you come in?"

Seth and Gillian walked inside, and though the apartment was quite small, it was severely clean and tidy. Seth said, "We're not here on church business. We need to ask you about the other day at the soup kitchen."

He nodded to Gillian, and she pulled the dress out of her oversized handbag. "Is this the dress you saw the other day?"

Transom took the dress, studied it a moment, then handed it back to Gillian. "I can't be certain. It might be, that's all I can say. You've got to understand, at first I didn't even realize what was happening. It was almost surreal, you know? I hadn't eaten for three days, and I had almost convinced myself I was hallucinating when I saw that poor woman stagger inside. By that time the woman who stabbed her was gone. I couldn't do a thing to stop it."

Gillian said softly, "It must have been a terrible thing for you to witness."

He nodded. "I chased after the murderer, but she turned the corner and by the time I got there, she was gone."

Seth said, "Are you certain it was a woman?"

"Well, she was in a dress, that pretty much proved it to me."

"No, what I mean is, could it have been a man in the dress?"

"A transvestite? I know they exist in the world, but I honestly didn't think there were any in Jackson's Ferry."

Gillian prodded, "We mean more like a disguise."

The young man thought a moment, then said, "I saw the dress, so naturally I assumed it was a woman. I never saw her face, though. I don't know, I just can't be sure."

Seth followed up by asking, "Anything else you saw that struck you as unusual or out of the ordinary?"

Transom shook his head, then said, "I thought it was a woman. She ran like a woman, anyway. I think. I'm sorry I can't be more definite."

Seth nodded. "Thanks, we appreciate the time. Sorry to bother you."

"No problem at all. If I should think of anything else, how should I contact you?"

"Just call Father Farabee, he'll know where to find me."

Back outside, Gillian said, "Well, that was another dead end."

"He remembered more than I would have. Take food away from me for three days and I'd be seeing dancing cheeseburgers on every corner. Speaking of food, I got hungry just listening to him. Why don't we go grab something to eat before we tackle Garska?"

Gillian looked surprised. "Are we still considering him after all we uncovered today?"

"He's got a slight build just like Jason, and there wasn't a positive identification on the dress. I'll feel better if we speak with him, too. If he has an alibi for last night, we can forget about him altogether and concentrate on Skyles."

All of the tables were taken at the Deli and Cream when Seth and Gillian got there. They took two stools at the bar and ordered across the lattice work that separated diners from the kitchen. The restaurant's pastel motif hadn't changed since the fifties, but the food was excellent.

As they drank their iced teas, Gillian said, "Would you say you're generally pretty happy with your life?"

"What in the world brought that question on?"

She took a sip, then said, "Since we've been investigating this case, you've begun to really come alive. I've never seen this side of you, and I can't help wondering if you should be doing police work instead of tree farming."

Seth patted his leg. "I've got this, remember?"

"Come on, Seth, you and I both know if you wanted to you could pass the physical. Have you ever thought about running against Harley Kline for sheriff?"

"Absolutely not. He's welcome to the grief and headaches that come with the job, and I'm not about to run against him. Not that I'd have a chance, anyway, Harley was born and raised in Jackson's Ferry, and a lot of people still think of me as an outsider."

"You've got a way with people, I can't imagine you not being elected."

Seth studied her a moment before commenting. In a soft voice, he said, "You're not trying to get rid of me, are you? If I were sheriff, my spare time would disappear. We both know I'd probably be putting in eighty-hour weeks."

"I just want you to be happy."

Seth touched her shoulder, then rubbed it gently. "I admit, there's some of the old racehorse still in me, but I've been a cop before, I don't want to do it again." The statement was perfectly true, as far as it went. Seth knew in his heart that he would forever tie being a cop with Melissa and the baby's deaths. Putting on a uniform again would bring all of that back, and he doubted he could handle it.

Gillian pushed a little harder. "You really love criminal justice, though, it's obvious."

Seth swirled the tea in his glass, staring idly at the whirlpool. "You know, I could always teach a class. If the college won't take me, I could work over at VCC. Adult education at the community college is really getting big lately."

Gillian nodded. "I'd be the first one in line to sign up for your class."

"You know enough to teach it with me. You know what, that's a great idea. Why don't we see if we could teach a basic 'The Law and You' class. We could get Allison Cole to lecture one night, maybe even the sheriff. What do you think?"

"It sounds like fun, but I'm not sure I'm qualified."

"You know more than most beat cops, your dad saw to that. It's settled, then, I'll look into it after this mess is over."

Seth's barbecue plate arrived, and two seconds later Gillian had her salad. After Seth took a bite, he couldn't keep the smile off his face. Gillian asked, "What's so funny?"

"Nothing in the world is funny about good Lexington-style barbecue. I'd offer you a bite, but I'm not willing to give up a single morsel of this." He looked at her salad with disdain. "Are you sure that's all you want?"

She patted his belly gently. "You're eating enough meat for both of us."

After lunch, they got to Garska's insurance office only to find the 'Closed' sign still on the door.

Seth said, "So he didn't come to work this morning. I wonder if he's still at home?"

"Do you think he went on another binge last night?"

Seth shook his head. "I doubt it. He's probably still suffering from his hangover from the night before. Never in my life have I seen anybody with a harder time holding his liquor."

They were just leaving when a young woman approached the building with a set of keys in her hand. She was obviously harried by the look on her face, and as she tried to fit the key in the lock, she dropped a large ring of keys on the ground.

Seth reached down and recovered them, then handed the ring back to her. She said, "Thanks, it's just been one of those days."

Gillian said, "Is Mr. Garska coming in today?"

The woman's face tightened as she said, "Haven't you heard the news?"

A dull ache crept into the pit of Seth's stomach. "What happened?"

"Mr. Garska was in a car accident last night. As he was leaving the wake for Mrs. Hobart, some drunk in a Lincoln blindsided him."

"Is he going to be okay?"

"It was touch and go last night, but they think he's going to pull through. As soon as they moved him out of intensive care I thought I'd better open the office up."

Seth asked softly, "When did it happen? Exactly."

She thought a moment, then said, "I think the police said it was around 6:45, but don't quote me on that. They called me at home just after eight, and I've been at the hospital all night." She had the door open, and they could hear the multiple lines ringing inside. "I've got to go. If you want, you can go see him during visiting hours tonight. He doesn't have many friends, so I know he'd be happy to see you."

Gillian asked, "Did the police say if he'd been drinking?"

The girl's eyes went wide. "Not that I know of. I understand Mrs. Hobart's death hit him hard, but I hadn't realized it was that bad."

"But you knew they were close, didn't you?"

Angrily, the girl said, "They were friends, okay? She used to stop by every now and then and take him out to lunch, and he'd go up to her place sometimes, but I don't care what anybody says, they weren't having an affair."

"You sound pretty sure of yourself."

"A man can hide a lot of things from his wife or his girlfriend that he could never hide from his secretary. I'd be willing to swear to it under oath." She looked inside, then said, "Listen, I really do have to go."

After she was safely inside, Gillian said, "I guess that eliminates him as a suspect."

"In Penny's death, anyway. I guess that means it all comes back to Skyles, doesn't it?"

Chapter 16

Gillian was surprised by Seth's intensity. It was almost as if his entire focus was now on Jason Skyles. She had to repeat herself three times before he heard her question.

"What did you say?"

"I said, now that we think Skyles killed his mother, what do we do about it? Shouldn't we tell the sheriff?"

Seth shook his head. "We don't have enough evidence to suit Harley Kline, especially since he's not willing to acknowledge the fact that Penny's death was anything but a suicide. If he won't accept that she was illiterate from us, what makes you think the dress we found in Skyles' studio will have any influence with him?"

"We can't just let him get away with it."

"There's no chance of that. I'm afraid we're going to have to take care of him ourselves."

Gillian looked at him steadily a few moments before trusting herself to speak. Was this the Seth she'd known through the last two years, a man full of compassion for his fellow man and a deep respect for the law? "Are you suggesting we play judge, jury and executioner?"

He looked as if he'd been slapped. "What? Of course not. All I'm saying is that it's up to us to get enough proof until even Harley's satisfied. Gillian, I thought you knew me better than that."

"So did I, but I've never seen you this intense."

He shrugged. "I can't help it, it's in my blood."

She rubbed his shoulder. "As long as you keep it in check we'll be fine."

"That's why you're here. I wish I knew where Skyles was. I think if I can just push him hard enough in the right direction, he might crack."

"What in the world makes you think that, Seth? You're the one who told me what a hard customer he was. He doesn't sound like the type of person who'd confess."

Seth said, "It's been my experience in the past that people want to talk, to brag about their cleverness, no matter how damning it is to them. Maybe he's doing just that right now. Can I borrow your telephone?"

Gillian handed it to him, and he dialed a quick number. "Paul, how's it going? You still playing tennis? Yeah, well, with this leg, I don't think I'd have much of a chance against you. Are you busy? I need you to check something out for me. The name is Jason Skyles. Could you check his file for me? I'm interested in the name of the bar he was arrested for D & D. Yeah, I'll hold." He held a hand over the receiver and said, "Paul Michaels at the police department. He's checking on Jason's rap sheet so I can see where he likes to drink. Chances are he still goes to the same bar, and if he's feeling the slightest remorse for what's been going on, he'll most likely be there. Hang on." Back to the phone, he said, "Yeah. Okay, listen thanks, Paul. I owe you a can of tennis balls. A case? I don't think so. Yeah, you're right, you can't blame a guy for trying. Catch you later."

As Seth handed the telephone back to Gillian, he said, "He likes to hang out at The Palace."

Gillian said, "Now why should we be surprised he favors topless bars?"

"Well, I've got to go check it out. Why don't I drop you off at your loft, then I'll let you know what happens."

"I don't think so, Buster. I'm going with you."

Seth tried to look innocent, failing miserably in Gillian's eyes. "You don't trust me?"

"You I trust. I just don't like the idea of you confronting Jason Skyles alone without having me around just in case."

"And it's got nothing to do with the half-naked women prancing around up on the stage?"

Gillian laughed. "If you find anything better than what you've got, be my guest."

"There's an empty offer, since you know it's impossible. Well, I never thought I'd say this to you, but let's go to the strip club."

Strip clubs were not Gillian's favorite places on earth, but not for the reason most people might have suspected. She'd long ago grown accustomed to skin, hers or others, and the exploitation factor of the establishment didn't bother her in the least. As a strong female, she knew it was the men there who were being exploited, not the women. It was a shame the girls made more money dancing than using their brains, but it was, in the end, their choice. In a way, it was appropriate: stunted women dancing for stunted men. The gene pool aspects made her shiver, but she doubted the two groups mated much.

No, the problems were more physical. Pounding music, staggering darkness interrupted by flashing lights and the stale clouds of cigarette smoke are what bothered her. She'd have to scrub twice to get the smell of the place off her.

It took a few seconds for her eyes to adjust to the insane lighting situation. It looked like they'd hit a dead-end, none of the scattered patrons was Jason Skyles. She was just about to tell Seth that when he touched her arm. "There he is, over by the pool table."

Sure enough, in one nook of the bar were two pool tables. Jason Skyles was playing by himself, and from the expression on his face he was losing badly.

As they walked over to the table, Gillian wondered how Seth would handle him. If things got out of hand, at least there was a massive brute behind the bar who most likely doubled as a bartender and a bouncer.

Seth surprised her by leaning over the pool table and grabbing the cue ball. Skyles looked at him with fierceness until he saw Gillian standing just behind Seth. He said directly to her, "Have you come in here to take me up on my offer to pose?"

Seth snapped, "Why should she bother, since you're sculpting her anyway?"

"So you're the ones who broke into my studio. I should

have you arrested."

Seth tossed the cue ball up and down, and Gillian noticed that he'd managed to attract the bartender's attention. He said, "I don't think so. We drove out there to talk to you, and we're both willing to swear that we heard someone inside who sounded like they were in trouble. It was our obligation to make sure no one was hurt." He added, "You really should be more careful when you lock up. You've got some valuable stuff out there. Equipment, I mean."

"What do you want? I'm not in any mood to deal with you, not with what's been happening."

Seth looked around the bar, letting his eyes linger on the stage. Gillian saw that a thin girl with exaggerated breasts was stripping off a bikini made of tiny confederate flags to the tune of "Dixie". From the attention she was getting from the customers, it appeared that the bar was full of true patriotic sons of the South. "You picked a pretty odd place to mourn."

Gillian started to say something to try to break the tension between the two men when she stifled herself. Seth was intentionally letting the steam build, hoping for an explosion of words.

"This is where I hang out, I'm comfortable here."

Seth looked around at the run-down decor. "Yeah, I can see that it's just like home."

"It is for me. I came here after that sorry excuse for a wake and had a going-away party for Vera myself, just me and all of my friends. I know she would have been mad, but she's not in any position to complain, is she? It's a shame, though, the two of us were starting to get along again."

Seth asked, "Can anybody prove you didn't slip away sometime during the party?"

Skyles pointed to the girl on stage, now sporting only one strategically placed flag. "Ask Betty. She was by my side the entire time. Let me ask you something. The police told Hobart that some homeless woman named Penny killed Vera."

"Yeah, well, unless she miraculously learned to write in a day, she couldn't have left that suicide note they found on her body."

Skyles slapped the table with a thunderous blow of his hand. "Son of a dog. I knew the cops were just looking for an easy way out of this."

There was no doubt in Gillian's mind the anger was real.

Skyles said hotly, "Why would I want to kill her, anyway? I didn't have a reason in the world for wanting her dead."

"You had a million of them, according to her insurance agent. Vera made you her sole beneficiary."

The news staggered Skyles against the table. Unless he'd missed his calling as an actor, he hadn't had a clue about Vera's changes to her policy.

Gillian wanted to say something to Seth, but before she could get his attention, he reached for Gillian's purse and pulled up the wrinkled dress they'd found in Skyles' studio. She'd probably have to buy a new handbag to get rid of the smell of the soiled garment. Seth waved the dress under Skyles' nose. "What would your buddies here think if they knew we found this in your studio? Did you wear it when you killed your mother?"

In an instant, Skyles was in Seth's face, his furious anger a palatable scent. "I didn't kill her. Now get that thing out of my face."

To his credit, Seth didn't back up an inch. "What are you trying to tell us, that you like walking around in women's clothes? Funny, I didn't take you for that type."

Skyles pushed the butt edge of his pool cue into Seth's chest, but Seth didn't flinch. "I don't know what you're talking about. I've never seen that thing in my life."

"So you just happened to have an old dress lying on top of your rag pile?"

"Did you look through the rest of my rags? I get them from the Salvation Army. They give me their cast-offs that are too ratty to sell. There's probably a dozen old dresses in that pile, along with shirts, pants, God knows what else. It's amazing what some people try to give away instead of just chucking in the garbage can." He eased his pool stick out of Seth's chest. "What's even odder are the things some people keep. I was over at Lex's house yesterday having a drink with her when we walked through her garage. She'd got crappy clothes in there I wouldn't even use in my studio."

Seth stared at him for ten seconds without saying a word.

Jason said, "Listen, I didn't kill my mother. Sure, we had some problems, but we were just managing to patch things up between us. I didn't want her dead."

Seth came out of his trance. "I know." He handed the cue ball back to Skyles. "Listen, I'm sorry we bothered you. I want your mother to get justice."

"Not any more than I do."

Seth said, "Come on, Gillian, we're going."

"Where to?"

Seth looked at her grimly. "To confront the real murderer."

Chapter 17

As they headed for the truck, Gillian asked, "Would you mind telling me where we're going? And if it's not too much trouble, I'd love to know who the murderer is."

Seth said, "Sorry, I wasn't trying to leave you out. It's just something Jason said in there that finally clicked."

"Seth Jackson, I want an answer, and I want it right now."

He nodded. "Lex Bascum. She's the one responsible for Vera's and Penny's deaths."

Seth felt Gillian eyeing him strangely. "Are you feeling okay? The last I heard, she wasn't even one of our suspects, and now you're claiming she's a double murderer. How'd you come to that conclusion?"

"Gillian, I should have seen it sooner, I was a cop long enough not to let what somebody tells me is true stand without confirmation. I just never gave Lex much thought."

"I still don't see it."

Patiently, Seth explained, "Okay, think back to the day Vera was murdered. We were at Lex's not long after, and what did we see?"

"She was packing some boxes in the garage."

"Right, but consider this. Lex is some kind of neat freak, there wasn't a spot of dust in that garage, and the boxes were brand new. Remember? There were a few still unfolded in one corner when we got there. So where'd the smudges on her face come from? I'm willing to bet she hadn't had a chance to check herself in the mirror before we got there. I bet you we'll find the dress she wore to kill Vera, too."

As he drove, Gillian said, "Come on, Seth, a few smudges of dirt don't make her a murderer."

"There's more. Remember she told us that her husband had been the one cheating on her, but when we saw him outside the funeral home, he told us Lex had been the one having an affair, and more importantly, that Vera had been the one to tell him about it. I call that motive enough for murder."

"How about Vera giving Penny her ring? Could Penny have been mistaken about that?"

"She wasn't sure who gave her the ring, remember? We just naturally assumed it was Vera, but it could have easily been Lex. The two of them looked close enough on the exterior, and if Lex stole the knife as she was shoving the ring in her hand, I doubt Penny would have noticed."

Gillian put a hand on his arm. "Slow down, you're making me nervous."

Seth glanced down at the speedometer and was surprised to find that he was going a good twenty miles over the posted 45 MPH speed limit. He started to ease off the gas, then pushed it down again. "I don't want to take a chance on Lex getting away. She told me herself she was leaving town today, and it'll be a lot harder to find her if she gets out of town." He grinned. "Besides, maybe a cop will catch us and have to follow us to her house. I think Lex might crack if she sees flashing lights coming her way."

"Just be careful, okay? If Lex was the one with Vera's ring, how did she get it in the first place?"

"Who would be in a better position to steal it than a woman who claimed to be her best friend? Vera could have been rinsing some dishes, taking a bath, who knows? It doesn't matter how she got it, it just matters what she did with it next."

Gillian nodded reluctantly. "I guess I can see you making a case against her for Vera's murder, but what reason in the world would she have to kill Penny? It looked like a perfect set-up to everyone but the two of us."

"I'm guessing Lex hadn't counted on Penny avoiding the police so long. She started to panic, then decided to take care of Penny herself. We'll have to ask her how she managed to get Penny up on that scaffold, but I'm willing to bet a handwriting expert will be able to prove Lex wrote that note.

She must have worried no one would find the body, so she put Penny's distinctive coat on until she was sure someone saw her. Dropping the coat on the street was brilliant. After that, she looked like anyone else milling around the square."

Gillian nodded. "I'll bet we walked right past her when we were looking for Penny."

Seth said, "I've got another idea. Check the glovebox, would you? I hope the batteries are still good."

Gillian found a small tape recorder inside. "When did you pick this up?"

Seth grimaced. "I wasn't going to say anything, but I've been thinking about writing a book." He waited for some kind of response from her; it was, after all, the first thing he'd kept from Gillian since they'd been together.

Gillian asked, "What's it going to be about?"

"I was thinking about doing something that would relate my educational experience with my time on the force, you know, comparing and contrasting academic life versus life on the street."

"It sounds fascinating."

He shrugged. "It probably would have been, but I haven't been able to get much further with it than buying that tape recorder."

She nodded. "I get it. We're going to try to trap Lex into a confession."

"Not that it would stand up in court, but if we've got her on tape, the sheriff will have to take her seriously as a suspect."

Finally, they pulled up into Penny's driveway. Her car was still there, Seth was relieved to see. He reached into his shoulder holster and pulled out his gun.

Gillian saw what he was doing and asked, "Do you really think you need that?"

"No matter how harmless she looks, there's no doubt in my mind that Lex has already killed two people. Do you think she'd stop at killing two more? You can stay out here if you want to. Call the sheriff if I'm not back in five minutes."

Gillian smiled bravely. "What, and let you have all the fun? I don't think so, I'm going with you."

Gillian started to reach for the doorbell when Seth caught her hand. "We don't want her to know we're here yet." He tried the knob and found it was locked.

"What now," Gillian asked.

"Let's check the patio door in back."

As they crept to the back of the house, Gillian peered into several windows. There was no sign of life anywhere. "Is there a chance she's not here?"

"Her car's in the driveway."

"Maybe she's over at Hobart's next door."

"If she is, then we'll wait for her."

Seth approached the rear deck door, tugged on the handle and was rewarded with it opening. Before he went through, he turned to Gillian, put a finger to his lips, then walked quietly inside.

Once they were both in, he heard a voice from the side command, "Drop your gun."

He pivoted slightly and saw that Lex had been hiding behind a massive armoire in the dining room. She had a .44 magnum pointed at them, so he didn't have much choice.

Seth dropped his gun to the padded carpet below.

Lex said, "Move over here. Both of you."

Seth did as he was told, searching for some way out of the mess he'd gotten them into. Had he slipped up coming in? No, there was no way he could have known she was hiding behind the armoire. Still, he'd taken a foolish risk by not calling the sheriff first. If he ever managed to get out of this, he'd have to stop thinking of himself as an active cop. It appeared that in the years since he'd left the force, he'd gotten rusty, somehow lost his edge. Though Lex held the gun, and with it all the cards, Seth wasn't ready to give up. She was making one mistake already, standing too close within his reach. If he could get her overconfident in her ability to handle the situation, he just might be able to get them out of this jam yet. He just hoped Gillian had hit the record button on the tape recorder before Lex had caught the two of them.

Trying to draw her out, Seth said, "You know, for an amateur you were pretty clever. You only made one or two mistakes, but they were whoppers."

He had to be careful in his goading. He wanted to keep her interested enough not to kill them until he could come up with a plan.

"Do you care to share them with me, since you're going to die anyway?" Lex asked.

Gillian spoke up. "One was the smudges on your face when we were here the first time. You're too much a neat-freak about your appearance to answer the door like that."

"I could have gotten dirty packing."

"How? The boxes were brand new, the clothing had been in storage, and you could eat off your garage floor. So where'd the dirt come from?"

"That's an awfully slim reason to accuse somebody of murder."

Seth spoke, calling Lex's attention back to him. "Okay, here's a real mistake. That suicide note Penny left was obviously a fake."

Lex looked outraged. "Come on, you've got to be kidding. 'Can't go on. I'm so sorry.' I thought it was rather touching."

"It would have been, if Penny wasn't illiterate. I'm afraid that tipped your hand." He had a sudden insight. "That writing was smudged. I'm willing to bet when the police check your eyebrow pencil they'll find a match."

"They would, if they'd ever think to check it. Thanks for the tip though, it was probably careless of me not to throw it away."

Gillian asked, "Why did you shoot at us at Seth's before we even started asking the hard questions?"

Lex shook her head in disgust. "Do you think I'm an

idiot? I knew why you came by my place the day Vera died. You were snooping, and I couldn't afford to have anybody looking too closely at my staged act."

Seth said, "So that's why you killed Penny. It was our fault."

"Don't give yourself so much credit. I was hoping the police would arrest her and I didn't figure anyone would believe a word she said. Then she double-crossed me by not getting caught. I must have prowled those streets for hours before I saw her scurrying like a rat. All it took was one look at my gun, and she did everything I told her to, from getting in my car to climbing up on those pallets and slipping the noose around her neck. It was almost too easy, like killing you two is going to be."

As she spoke, Seth saw Gillian out of the corner of his eye knock a candelabra off the dining room table. As Lex pulled her gun off Seth to point it at Gillian, Seth made his move, diving the three feet to where Lex stood and grasping for the gun.

It exploded just as his hands reached for her.

His ears were still ringing from the explosion when the sheriff came in. Though he had a pounding headache, he'd refused to relinquish the gun he was holding on Lex until Kline himself got there.

Lex had been steadily assaulting him with profanity from the moment Gillian dialed 911 to the sheriff's arrival. Seth was secretly glad Lex had broken down finally, telling them everything she'd done, almost bragging about the fact that she'd outsmarted just about everyone but Seth and Gillian. That led to another string of curses, and the woman's shouts weren't helping his headache.

After she was cuffed and led away, Sheriff Kline said, "You took an awful chance not calling me in on this."

Seth nodded. "I know, but I didn't really have anything like concrete proof. I'd planned to trick her into a confession, but she managed to get the jump on me."

Kline patted his shoulder. "Don't let that get you down. She fooled a lot of us."

Gillian stepped forward. "You might want to listen to this. It's got some interesting information on it about what really happened." Before Kline could say a word, Gillian added, "We know it's probably not admissible, but it will surely give you some new places to look."

Seth smiled at her. He had made the leap for Lex's gun more for the fear he felt for Gillian's life than his own. He would have taken the bullet for her, in fact he'd meant to do just that if it had been needed, but Lex pulled her arm up at the last second, a reaction to his movement that had sent the bullet harmlessly into the ceiling.

"Are you doing okay?" Gillian asked softly.

"If I can get rid of this headache, I'll be fine."

Gillian smiled slowly. "I know just the thing to take care of it."

Chapter 18

After giving statements to the sheriff's men, the two of them ended up back at Gillian's loft. As she rubbed his neck, Seth said, "This isn't exactly what I had in mind for headache relief."

She laughed as she rubbed the muscles harder. "I thought that was supposed to be the perfect excuse not to have sex."

He sat up and said, "Actually, recent studies have shown that it can actually improve a headache."

Gillian slid onto his lap. "I'm guessing you'd like to test that particular theory. Well, if you're willing to take the chance of making it worse, I'm game."

Later, Gillian asked gently, "Well, did it help your headache?"

"What headache?"

She tossed her pillow at him as she got up. "You're incorrigible. I believe I've told you that before."

He smiled as he said, "Where are you going, anyway?"

"I'm calling Hank and Claire and see if they still want us to visit. Big Pine Key sounds wonderful to me."

Seth jumped up out of bed. "If we drive straight through, we should be on the beach this time tomorrow."

"I was thinking more along the lines of waiting until after the weekend."

Seth said, "And take a chance on something else delaying our trip? No way. Pack what you need, then we'll go. We can leave the truck here."

"Isn't there anything you want to take along for yourself?"

"No, I don't plan to wear much more than my bathing suit and what I've got on. Anything else I need I'll buy once I'm down there."

As they were walking out the door, the telephone started

to ring. Gillian reached for it when Seth took her hand.

"Do you really want to take a chance on answering that?"

They could still hear the telephone ringing as they walked out of the loft and into the cool May air.